Chuggi Files

A story of a dog with swag and anger issues.

Samarth Gupta

BlueRose ONE.com
Stories Matter
NewDelhi • London

BLUEROSE PUBLISHERS
India | U.K.

BlueRose ONE
Stories Matter
NewDelhi • London

For permissions requests or inquiries regarding this publication, please contact:

BLUEROSE PUBLISHERS
www.BlueRoseONE.com
info@bluerosepublishers.com
+91 8882 898 898
+4407342408967

ISBN: 978-93-93386-42-7

Cover design: Shreemoi Saha
Typesetting: Sagar

First Edition: January 2025

"This book is dedicated to Lord Ganesha, as it is only through his blessings that I was able to write it. I also dedicate it to my dear son, Mantra, and to all pet owners who love their pets, no matter the circumstances. I want to express my heartfelt gratitude to my wife, Saumya, for her unwavering support, as well as to my family members. A special thank you goes to Nihit Mohan for his guidance throughout this journey."

Introduction

Having a dog is every boy's dream. It was my dream, too; it became our dream after marriage. Dreams do come true, but at a cost; my parents always said no to pets, and believe me, they were right. Having a pet is a big responsibility and involves many sacrifices and headaches. But every good thing comes after much pain and struggle; the same is true about having a pet. The love they give you is truly unique and unconditional; it doesn't matter to your dog whether he sleeps on a cot or with you on your bed, whether he lives in a big house or a small apartment. He loves you the same. For him, you are his entire world.

Every relationship changes with time, sometimes good or bad, be it with your parents, friends or spouse. But not with your pet. He will love you and always see you the same way; for him, you are the best person in the whole world. Your social status, economic status, or even current relationship status doesn't matter to him. All he wants is love.

Contents

One

THE WAIT AT THE AIRPORT

"There is still one hour before the boarding starts. We request your patience and are extremely sorry for the discomfort. Please collect your snacks from the front counter at gate no. 6." The aeroplane staff announced.

I was at the 'Netaji Subhash Chandra Bose International Airport, Kolkatta'. My flight was delayed by more than one hour. Frankly, waiting at the airport is one of the most unpleasant experiences in life. The airport authorities think that by having excellent infrastructure and opening a mall at the airport, the passengers will like the experience. But, there is not much to it. After shelling thousands of rupees on the flight, why would you go to buy a watch? On top of that, travelling via flight is a dull journey. And yes, that smile of the beautiful air hostess is fake and definitely not for you. On top of it, airports are usually far from the city, so you leave two hours prior and then you need another two hours to check in, all this for an hour's journey! Secondly, everything is so costly in this mall. On top of this, the airlines inside give us their five-star food, the famous cold refrigerated sandwich and cuppa Maggie.

And finally, why don't airport authorities provide more sleeping seats? You can't even sleep at the airport like you can at the railway station. As kids, when we used to wait for the train in the summer heat with those Chacha Chaudhary comics, was so fun!

I asked one of the air hostesses; she promptly replied, "Sir, kindly wait for a few minutes; the boarding will start soon." Then I saw a support ground staff member, the techie guy with earpieces; these guys working backstage, you should talk to. He was wearing a blue jacket and a fabulous pair of cheap sunglasses. The guy had some swag. He told me very excitedly that there was some problem with the front wheel and it wasn't turning. Also, there was a high chance the plane might get cancelled; he said this sentence smiling, showing his tobacco-stained teeth.

I was now having second thoughts. I thought about the episode of Friends where Pheobe was boarding the plane, and she made up the story that there was a problem with the left Philangee; I felt like the other passenger sitting beside her. I'm not too fond of air travel, and all this waiting made me anxious and nervous; I started imagining the worst scenario when the plane landed: the front wheel got jammed, the plane skidded, the gate was not opening, and there was fire. I jumped in and saved all the passengers and air hostesses. They smiled at me and thanked me, with everyone trying to take a selfie.

But imagination also has its limit; my wife quickly invaded that imagination with her call, and I was back with my anxieties. I was getting bored; after all, there was a limit to how much I could see on social media, and my thumb was paining. Also, people these days don't talk to each other. I saw a beautiful girl with straight hair and a round face buying coffee. Her demeanour exuded a blend of nervous excitement and determination. Dressed in a smart blazer and pressed trousers, her attire reflects a sense of professionalism, like she is going for an interview or an important meeting.

However, being a married man, I defocused myself from her and thought I was better off oogling at the Instagram models. Getting bored, I picked myself up and moved towards the book counter.

The store was packed, too, as two more planes were delayed. The same girl that caught my eye was now buying some chocolates; she was there with her friends. I tried looking for a book but could not decide what to read. Waiting for my flight to take off has just drained all my energy.

She seemed a bit too talkative, chatting with her friends and laughing, still in her twenties with all the young energy; I assumed she must have just started working, that's why she was so excited about everything; she was in her Go Girl phase! I tried focusing on the books, but she was constantly saying something or the other. Then, she lost interest in the chocolates and started looking for a book; the store was small, so she stood next to me. It made me more uncomfortable. Somehow, around beautiful girls, our teenage brain just gets activated.

I picked up a copy of the book "Marley and Me." She saw it and exclaimed, "Wait, is that 'Marley and Me'? It's my all-time favorite book! It's hard to find in stores these days. When I was a kid, my family and I watched the movie, and I loved that sweet dog, Marley. After watching the movie, I wished for a dog, but my parents didn't allow it. Now that I'm working and independent, I plan to get a Labrador as a pet very soon."

I didn't ask for these details, and as I was already in a bad mood and her constant talking irritated me so much, I looked down and murmured to myself, " Ohh, please! Leave the poor lab alone,"

And she heard it.

"What do you mean, Mr, who are you to comment?"

"Ohh, I didn't mean.."

"Hey, how can you talk to a woman like that." Her friend angrily jeered at me.

"I was muttering under my breath; if you feel I have offended you, I am extremely sorry." I became extremely nervous. The adolescent mind just gave way to the 2-year-old Dad. I got uneasy; I would be in trouble if the girl got angry.

"I am a family man, and I have my dog. Please, I am sorry."

"Okay, Okay, Uncle, don't be worried... So you said you have a dog at home? What's his breed?"

Desi! It was the first word that came to my mind; however, to sound a bit classy, I said. "It's a mixed breed, ma'am."

"Which breeds?"

I didn't know that because, as I said, he was Desi or a local Indian breed. But I always had this answer ready: "German Shepherd and Husky."

"Ohh, he must be cute." Said her friend.

"Can we see his photo?" The talkative girl asked.

"Ohh, yes." And I showed them his latest photograph

"He is handsome. What's his name?"

"Chuggi," I replied.

"Such an unusual name, by the way, you are travelling to? " the talkative girl asked.

"Mumbai by 6B534, it's delayed."

"I am travelling by the same plane. It's so boring waiting here. Well, by the way, why didn't you want me to have a dog? When you already have one." The girl asked again.

We had come out of the bookstore, my seat was gone, and this girl was now making me really uncomfortable.

"Having a dog is a big responsibility."

I left them and found one seat in the corner, and my mind raced in all directions. The last few months had been so hectic that I had forgotten everything that had happened, and that one question brought all the memories back. I felt guilty, angry, and worried at the same time. I realised my dog had grown old and would not be with me forever. I took one last glance at that girl. People should consider having pets seriously; they are not some playthings.

My mind started playing the scenarios in my head, and I got sucked into an overthinking loop; Needing a distraction, I opened my office diary and began drafting an urgent letter for my boss.

At this stage of my life, doing office work and scrolling on social media are my only sources of distraction.

Dear Mr Chuggi.

I meant Mr. Shrivastav; my mind was still on Chuggi. Because of Chuggi, my family has been on a roller coaster for the last year.

So why not write a letter to my dog? Mr Shrivastav can wait.

I know you can't understand this, but I still want to say that I am sorry.

I am sorry for all those days when we left you at home for hours daily when we had to go to work.

I am sorry for all those nights when we returned from our offices late and you were eagerly waiting for us. We went out to parties and movies again, and you had to wait for us on those lonely nights.

I am sorry that we left you at those dreaded dog hostels while we went to enjoy, travel and recreate ourselves.

I am sorry for neglecting you after Kabir.

I am sorry we couldn't find time to train or play with you. I know you waited for me to throw the ball every night and thrash that bottle after dinner.

You are the best dog we know; I hope we could have been better parents.

Please forgive me.

Yours lovingly

Hoooman

Suddenly, that talkative girl appeared out of nowhere and sat near me. We are so used to being in our zone alone with our phones, heads down, mindlessly scrolling through social media that anyone talking to us suddenly in real life, even a beautiful girl, can make us nervous. I was also sitting happily with my sad thoughts, and here she came and said, "Hey, I am a better person and a responsible adult who just started working in a big MNC; who are you to say I can't have a dog."

"Ehh, ok, I am sorry, Miss?

"Meenakshi." She replied quickly.

"Hi, I am Rishi."

"Okay, but why did you say that earlier? You don't know anything about me; how can you be so judgemental?"

"And I have left you all alone after that; why are you interrogating me? It's your life, your decision." I replied, getting a bit irritated.

"Actually, I am still not sure I want to do it."

"So leave it."

"But I want a dog as a pet, and I always wanted to have one. And my parents didn't allow me. Someday, I might get married, and if my husband didn't want to have a dog, then what? I live by the principle, You get this life once, so I need to have all the experiences before I die."

"Then go do Bunjee jumping, travel and run, play whatever the hell you want to do; why are you after the life of a poor thing," I said angrily.

"I also want more likes on my Instagram page; you see, I have also thought about the name of our page, The Adventures of Pintu and Minu. I am planning to get a male dog; I follow, you know, all the famous pet influencers like...." She continued as though she didn't even hear me.

Now, to have some likes on Instagram, people want a dog. I had to interrupt her.

"Do you know your biggest challenge with a pet?"

"To get him to walk?"

"Ohh, that's just the basic." Think more.

"Getting him to vet?"

"Hmm, yes and no, depends on your dog's temperament, still think?"

"Where to leave him when I am out? You know I have already seen a good day boarding."

"Okay, I will give you that; you had that sorted, but will you leave him there daily?" I replied

"No. Only when I will go out of the city." She replied

"So you said that you worked in MNC. Which sector?

"Software." She replied

"And which city do you work in?" I asked

"Mumbai." She replied

"Where is the office located," I asked

She looked at me suspiciously and said, "Why do you want to know? Anyway, my office is located in BKC."

"Okay, and tell me the distance between your office and home."

"This flight is sooo irritating. It's 23 Kilometers, and I take the local train from Thane. "

"Ohh, so this means you leave at 08:00 am and return at 08:00 pm. on good days?" I asked.

"No," she replied silently.

"Then?"

"I leave at 7:30 am, take an auto to the station, and then I have to take the 08 o'clock local, or else it gets too rushy. The ladies' compartment is especially full. I considered taking a first-class ticket, but it's so costly compared to second-class..."

"When do you come back?" I had to interrupt her local.

"Well, by 09:00 pm, but you see, you don't get an auto in the return time from BKC to Kurla. These Auto drivers don't wanna go; they are some sort of cartel. It's so frustrating, so I leave the office around..."

"Wait, 09:00? Are you nuts? When will the poor thing go to the toilet? Whom will he see the whole day? And if you

can't come then what will happen? Then one day, he will become sick, and you will get irritated and leave him, or worse, he will become aggressive and do some harm."

In anger, my letter pad fell from my lap, and she picked it up.

"I get your point." And she picked up the letter pad.

I quickly snatched my pad from her.

"Wait, Chuggi is the name of your dog, right? Why are you writing this letter to your dog as though he will understand?"

"Well... it's a long story."

"And our flight is still delayed by an hour; please tell me why this letter? And it seems something happened, that's why you are so angry. Please tell me what happened; it will be helpful. Your dog seemed so cute." She said, making puppy eyes.

As a man, saying no to those eyes would be inhuman.

"And, if Chuggi could reply, what would he say?"

"Hmm..."

"Please, it will be helpful for me to decide." She insisted

"Okay, fine. He would probably say."

Dear Hooman

"Bhoww love u....."

Lick rear lick... "Love u again hooman; take me for a walk, hooman."

"Take me out without a leash, you hooman. Don't be scared. Me there to protect you, hooman."

"No dog will come near you hooman, I am the alpha.."

"Hooman, just one thing.."

"Don't leave me ever.... Bowwow."

Yours

Grrr... Cat seen bhoww kill her.... Bhoww Chuggi

She laughed. "Okay, please tell me what happened. I want to know everything. And by the way, what will be the biggest challenge I will face with the dog?"

"let's see, hmm...The answer to this question is a lot complicated. Yes, I asked you this, but now, thinking about it, it's so much and so less. Walking, barking, maybe everything or nothing."

"What do you want to say? Your statement doesn't make any sense."

"I don't know. I suppose I will have to tell you my story to answer my question. If you had met me a. year ago, my answer would have been different."

"What happened a year ago?"

"Well, my happy life got bitten, and everything changed."

Two

THE BITE
ONE YEAR AGO

"Bowww wowww", followed by a shrill "Ouch!" A loud shriek came straight from the room where Mehrunisa was working; something horrible had happened.

Chuggi got loose by mistake, and unfortunately, our house help Mehrunisa was bitten by him. She became the second victim of dog bites in our home. As you may know, dog bites can be pretty dreadful. They can leave a nasty scar and cause a lot of pain and discomfort for the victim. Not only the risk of contracting rabies but also the emotional trauma of the bite can be quite overwhelming.

The first thought that came to my mind was whether or not my 7-month-old boy Kabir was safe. He was in the same room as she was working, but luckily, nothing had happened to him. Several thoughts stormed through my head as we took her to the hospital. Like why did we even keep this dog? The pain in Mehrunisa's eyes, the horror.

Our lives became chaotic after my wife became pregnant with Kabir. Dog baby, and recently, I had been on many tours where I wasn't even at home most of the time, and as a result, we were stressed to our limits; then, on top of all that, this happened.

It scared us to hell. Chuggi has been avoiding Kabir; what should we make of it? We know he had never bitten anyone in our close relations, and he was always suspicious of outsiders, but the family was family to him.

But this is our kid, so this incident changes everything. Can we take a risk with this dog?

Sitting outside the emergency room, I thought, what should I do? There are no decent animal shelters in the city; shall I leave him far off? Or worse, shall this dog be put to sleep? My eyes filled with tears as these thoughts cropped up in my head.

I knew one thing was certain: I love my dog like my kid, and this behaviour was our fault.

Three

AND THAT'S HOW IT ALL STARTED.

"So, that's what happened." Meenakshi said, "But dogs are supposed to be suspicious of strangers, and you want a dog that protects his owners, and such incidents always happen with pet owners. Also, your dog is a mix; I am getting a Lab, a pedigree breed."

"So you think all Labs just sit, grow fat and don't bite? Just google, and you will find plenty of such incidents, and well-biting is just one part of the story."

"May I ask you one more thing?

"Yes,"

"Why did you get this dog?"

"Well, my reasons were similar to yours."

" And here you are saying no to me."

" That's why I am saying No."

"Still, why?"

It was the second year of college when I met this beautiful girl and fell in love at first sight—waiting for the text reply and trying to find the message's hidden meaning. Meeting for small dates, She smiled, I smiled, and I was struck with the love arrow. For her, I was just a friend, but for me, she was my everything.

I got into the friend zone, texted more, met her at the bus stop, gave her chocolates, and smiled. Texted her more and found some competition, but I kicked them out. She texted me late at night on trips in front of her father's watchful eyes. My feelings soared, but even a year later, I was still her good friend; when I expressed my feelings, she repeated those golden words Anne-Marie said in her song FRIENDS: "You say you love me, I say you crazy. We are nothing more than friends."

Lonely heart, I roamed in the streets of my city as she was nowhere to be seen, but as fate would have it, a year later, I was in a relationship.

Now she had a dog at her home, and I had a dog at my home, and we fell in love, married, and started our lives in the beautiful and holy city of Haridwar.

It has been over four beautiful months since we married. Love was in the air, and we were adjusting to our new lives in my company-provided house. Every evening, we went out on outings and had dinner with friends. We were young and carefree, and given that we both had dogs at home, we thought having a small puppy running around here would be fun. Our first instinct was to get a Husky!

But knowing that dogs are a big responsibility, we decided not to go with this plan. Also, my mother's dog, Sheru, was about to shift with me very soon, as it was getting hard for her to manage him. Apart from all this, we both are in transferable jobs, so getting a puppy was out of the question.

But you see, as fate would have it, we will get a Husky in a German Shepherd's skin and with a wolf's temperament.

Life has a unique way of fulfilling our desires. One cold night in January, my partner and I were snuggled up in our blankets, watching adorable dog videos of Huskies on YouTube. It was raining heavily outside, and we had no idea that a pleasant surprise awaited us the next day.

As I left for my office the next day, I saw a tiny, frail puppy at my stairs. Someone had left him there in a box the night before, and as soon as he saw me, he wagged his tail and started following me. The next morning, I saw him again, and he again followed me. The kids in our building named him 'Tuffy'. He was the size of a palm, probably just over 15 days old.

The next evening, when my wife 'Radhika' and I returned from a party, we saw him cuddling up in the corner of the stairs. He was in a dire state, and it was again freezing that night. It would be tough for him to survive the night, so we took him in.

We thought we would leave him the following day so the kids in the building could play with him. And we did just that. He again followed me to my car.

That night, we brought him home again. We played with him and couldn't send him back this time. He was so cute and tiny that he could easily fit in one of my wife's boots!

Our parents thought it was ridiculous and protested, so to appease them, we decided to get this pup healthy and then give him up for adoption.

Then, one day, he stopped eating and got the Pargo disease. We took him to the vet. He said his condition was deplorable; he immediately injected him. The poor little puppy was on drips! And I had to go to the vet for three straight days.

Taking his care and his ultimate cuteness made us fall in love with him. So we decided that this dog was staying!

Four

THE DUDE, DOGGY!

"That's such a cute and romantic story." Meenakshi said smilingly, "Now you have such a cute story of a dog. Let me also have one." She said jokingly.

Then, her friends joined us; luckily, they were on a different flight, which was running on time.

"Uncle's story is interesting", one of them jeered at me, and they all started giggling.

I became nervous; why did I agree to all of this? I was better off sitting alone; I didn't know this girl. There is no reason to share my story with her except that she is a beautiful girl, but this doesn't matter that much at this stage of my life.

But then, when was the last time someone was interested in my story? We all live our own stories where we are the hero/heroine, fighting our battles. So much happens in our lives, but most of us don't get to share our stories; everyone wants to tell their own story, but no one wants to listen. As we become middle-aged, we lose our friends, and work becomes everything; we fight so many battles daily with our boss and coworkers, at home, with money, the daily commute, our dreams, and aspirations. Only our partners know, but as they are in their own story, they don't know the actual story.

"This is for the passengers travelling to Mumbai by flight 6B 534, which is further delayed by one hour. We are extremely sorry for the inconvenience." The airline authorities announced.

" It seems our flight is not leaving soon ".

"So please continue...".

Parents are happy seeing their kids doing something they couldn't do. It's their innate desire that their kid fulfil their dreams. For example, they couldn't be a doctor, so they want their kid to be one.

Well, I felt something like that for my dog. Not in a conventional way; after all, he is just a dog.

As Chuggi grew into a beautiful black colour dog, he started looking more like a Husky with the colour of a German Shepherd. He was hyperactive, always running in the house. There was occasional chewing of shoes and sandals, doing all the usual things that an adolescent dog usually does.

But there was something else. Even at seven months, my dog had a badass nature, like he was some doggy dude. He was fearless, like a wolf.

One winter morning, Chuggi was nicely sleeping on his cot on the balcony, enjoying the sun; a group of ten monkeys came and sat on a mango tree just at the side of the balcony. As soon as the group arrived, Chuggi started barking, and he barked his heart out. The monkeys were in a mood of mischief, so a few monkeys came down to slap him, but nothing would stop him; he would still bark. Finally, he caught one of the monkeys, and we had to intervene. Luckily, the monkey didn't get hurt that much. Chuggi was also all right.

Still a seven-month-old pup, he showed us He is a Tough Guy.

With this attitude, the female dogs started noticing him, and he quickly became a ladies' man. He ensured all the male dogs in the area knew who the boss was. He could easily handle two dogs double his size at eight months old! Even when he was sick and couldn't get up from his bed, he would still bark his heart out if he saw another dog or a stranger.

Above all, our colony had many trees and was in a picturesque location with many monkeys and street dogs. It was the best place for him to use his skills.

And just like that, he grew up to be a big, beautiful dog. Diwali was around the corner, and we had to go home; it was our first Diwali after marriage. We have managed somehow, but now we will be gone for eight days. Since we were not from Haridwar and we didn't have our own house, where to leave Chuggi was our first challenge. Haridwar is a small town, so our choices were very few. Luckily, after much searching, we found a nice place named Kennel Aashirwad at Doiwala, a small town between Haridwar and Dehradun.

And we left him there with a heavy heart.

"Okay, I get it; leaving a dog is hard. Luckily, I live in Mumbai, and many Kennels offer a pick-and-drop facility for pets there."

"Yes, Miss, but we didn't have that facility in Haridwar; it was our luck even to find a kennel that provided a boarding facility for dogs ..."

A young boy was sitting next to us. I didn't notice him at first; he seemed busy on his phone with a book on his lap waiting to be read. Suddenly, he looked at me. He must be around 5'3" and had a fair complexion with small eyes.

"So, sir, you have a dog?"

"Yes. And you are?"

"Hi, I am Aditya; I am also on the flight to Mumbai."

"Hi, Meenakshi here." Meenakshi jumped in and smiled at him.

"Hi...." said Aditya with a big smile on his face.

"Okay.... Coming back to my story...." I overlooked him and continued.

It was our first Diwali after marriage. We were meeting with friends and family, roaming on those known streets, and meeting a friend here and there. Mom was angry. She didn't want us to go anywhere; she wanted us to be close to her. Ahh, there is no place on earth like your hometown.

But even here, our thoughts were always on Chuggi, like how he was what he was doing.

When we returned, I asked the caretaker how he was. Did he eat properly? As it was his first time away alone, was he upset all the time? The caretaker said, "Bhaiji, your dog owned my kennel; he was like a don. No dog, even big ones, dared to do anything to him. My girl named him "Chuggi Anna". And he is so ready for mating; he also made a bitch fall in love with him, a Saint Bernard female twice his size! She was also there for boarding. And both of them cried and made a lot of noise through the night. It was very difficult to sleep, and because of these two, my other dogs started to bark and cry."

Also, he learned a little trick: Male dogs usually put dust on it after pee to mark their territory, and the dust also carries off their pheromones to far places. This ensures the other male dogs know a new boss is here and signals to all the babes that their hero is here. Now Chuggi, being him, made a dust storm after every pee!

The mating season for dogs was also on in our colony, and he found a new admirer Langdi! She was a beautiful black and white dog, but some stupid kid wrapped a firecracker on her feet, and her foot got damaged, and she walked like a lame dog. Hence the name. Well, she was in heat, and she just wanted him.

Our colony had many male dogs, and everyone was after her. She would come to our flat and sit in front of the gate every night that season, and Chuggi would cry from inside, scratching the door for inside and trying to open it like lost lovers desperate to meet each other. All this was happening at 2 a.m. in the night! A few dogs would follow her, and Chuggi would bark frantically from inside. It was becoming a headache, and the neighbours started to complain.

Then, one day, she came up a bit early; I was a bit careless. The door wasn't locked from the inside, and Chuggi stood up to see her; the door opened, and he ran like a bullet, not towards her, but towards the other dogs sitting downstairs. A huge fight broke out. Luckily, his leash was still on him; I pulled him back and rushed straight home. We thought he was hurt. But hmm, no, he had bitten not one but two dogs!

This was the beginning of Chuggi's violent streak. His response would always be the same towards another male dog, even on normal days. Here, I think we made the worst mistake. We didn't correct, train, or even socialise him; even in a sinister way, I felt proud that this dog was such a badass. Something that I never was.

I have always been rule-abiding, in the office or at home. I seldom fight or get into an argument. I like my peace. But at times, it leads to me getting pushed around. Radhika is also the same, but she is still bolder. So when

I saw this dog doing this, I couldn't correct him. I know this sounds ridiculous, but that's what I did.

And it would cost me so dearly.

Coming back to the story. We didn't let Chuggi mate that season. Anyway, some other guy got lucky, and Langdi gave birth to a beautiful all-black female, and the colony kids named her Kali.

But still, her admiration for Chuggi didn't go away, and she, now accompanied by her puppy Kali, continued happily following him.

Kali was even a bigger fan of Chuggi, so in the next season, when Kali reached puberty, both these mother-daughter duo would follow me on walks with Chuggi. In that mating season, there were many suitors for the mother-daughter duo, but both followed Chuggi. And the ruckus just increased.

The dude was enjoying the undivided attention of two bitches.

"Where are you from?" Aditya interrupted me

"I am from..."

"Not you; where are you from Meenakshi?"

I felt a little hurt but overlooked it.

"I am actually from Bikaner, but my family shifted to Kolkata a long time back."

"Okay, that's why you seem a bit different. Can I ask you one more thing?"

"Yes."

"Did it hurt?"

"What?" I said, looking bewildered.

" I am not asking you."

Meenakshi looks up, confused. "Uh, did what hurt?"

"When you fell... from the airport ceiling. Because, you know, you're like, uh, an angel? ...or something?

I pretended not to hear this question; a slap was probably coming straight towards him soon. And that's why he wanted to listen to my story.

Meenakshi laughed " Wow, that's, um, creative. I think it's 'fell from heaven', though."

"Oh, yeah! Right! Classic mix-up. I get my cheesy lines all tangled up when I see someone... distractingly pretty."

Meenakshi raised an eyebrow and said, "So... do you use this line often?"

"Only when I'm sitting next to a potential 'flight risk'. Get it? Flight? Airport?"

That's too cheesy; now a slap is confirmed.

But Meenakshi smirked. "That one was slightly better. Slightly."

"Well, shall I continue?" I asked, looking at Meenakshi.

"Ohh, please," Meenakshi said, smiling at Aditya.

"One more thing, you could have left Chuggi, let the poor guy have some action."

"Well, I couldn't; how can I explain it? It would have looked awkward."

"He is a dog dude," Aditya said with a smirk, and Meenakshi giggled.

I looked at him and thought, why was I even telling him this story? If Meenakshi hadn't been here, this would have been the end of the story. Or there would have been no story at all.

I gathered my thoughts and continued.

It was such a headache for me to deal with the attention that Chuggi was getting from girls. I had to carry sticks to shoo away the dogs. Besides, Chuggi would pull the leash so hard that it was almost impossible to control him when he wanted to pee and mark his territory. Whenever he saw a male dog, he would get so angry that he would bark frantically and pull with all his strength, making it even harder to manage him. It was becoming increasingly challenging to keep him under control.

Apart from the Langdi and Kali, he enjoyed occasional attention by a male dog named Kalu, who used to follow him and roll down in front of him. But Chuggi, being a dominant alpha dog, just bit him on one of his belly rolls when I wasn't watching him, and that was the end of their friendship.

"Hey, are you listening to me?" Meenakshi was scrolling through her Instagram feed, and Aditya was looking at her hands. It was now very clear where his interest lay. And definitely, it wasn't my story. I couldn't blame him for a boy; nothing could compete with a beautiful girl.

"Shall I stop? If my story is that boring."

"No, I was looking at this reel of a beautiful golden retriever. See how her owner writes these cute captions, 'I wanna Chimken,' as though he could say anything. What would your dog say if he could about this situation? You can also make a reel this way and get followers."

"Hmm."

" I saw your Instagram page. Actually, it just now showed you as a suggestion. How does it even know I am talking to you?"

"Yeah, its algorithm is really spooky," I added.

"My one post gets more likes than your following numbers and followers combined." She derided me.

A girl is checking out my Instagram page; finally, getting a cute dog paid off. But my dream was shattered when my phone rang, and my wife's photo appeared on it.

"Ahmm, hmm ok, see you, bye", and the call ended. She gave me a to-do list, and I was back to reality."

"My Instagram page is by the name Cool_Aditya_95," Aditya said to Meenakshi. One of her friends started giggling.

"So?" Meenakshi said

"Just saying." he started looking here and there.

And just like that, my mind flashed with images of Chuggi doing crazy zoomies in that tiny apartment and my wife's giggles. Man, those were good times. I can't help but wonder what Chuggi would have thought about all those shenanigans.

"Bhow ,love Hooman."

"PEE wanna go, Hooman."

"Nice PEE smell, beautiful girl, Sex!"

"Other dog, me alpha Bhow Bhow I bite he run."

"Hooman go outside. I wait. Sit on the sofa. Love sofa. No sit in front of Hooman".

"Bone Bone, I love Bone."

"Hooman Hooman I love Hooman. Any other Hooman comes near Hooman, I bite other Hooman!"

"Hate Pigeons, Hate monkeys love u, Hooman."

Five

THE HOUSE SWITCH

"I liked how you talk," Aditya said, looking at Meenakshi.

Meenakshi blushed. "Who's mine??"

"No, No uncle's," Aditya said hurriedly.

"The name is Rishi! And the real story is about to start." I continued hurriedly.

"I think his story is like the show 'How I Met Your Mother'; it's just too long, and probably we will not meet any mother either," Aditya said.

"Shh, I want to know what happened." Meenakshi intervened.

"Yes, please continue. We don't have time to wait for nine seasons." Said Aditya smiling at Meenakshi. My mind played the recently famous song used in Instagram reels

with the caption "Boys": "I-I-I got this feeling, yeah, you know, Where I'm losing all control, cause there's magic in my bones".

From the corner of my eye, I saw an air hostess wearing a stunning blue uniform sitting about ten feet away from us. She looked interested in our conversation, glancing at us a few times. Her tailored attire emphasised her graceful demeanour, and she wore a neatly pinned scarf and carefully styled hair that framed her radiant face. Suddenly, she walked over and sat next to us.

This is getting interesting.

"So let's begin again, so as I was saying..." I resumed my story

To summarise our several challenges with our pet dog in those early days. Every morning, when we wanted to cuddle, he needed to go out to pee. We felt bad for staying out late for parties and movies as he waited for us. He would bark at every stranger, which resulted in fewer guests visiting us. During the mating season, he would cry and stay awake, which caused complaints from our neighbours. This happened more often during winter when I wanted to sleep longer.

Additionally, he would bark loudly whenever we had to leave him alone at home to go outside for fun activities or to relax. Interestingly, he never cried when we left for work. In short, he had no issues if we left at 10:00 am and returned at 5:00 pm. However, if we went at 5:00 pm or 5:00 am, he would express his sadness through his cries.

Despite all these challenges, we loved him dearly, and every moment spent with him in that house was a blessing filled with love.

Everything was going great, and all our affairs were settled. However, life had a different plan for us, throwing us a curveball. It was as if life was giving us a mixed drink of lemonade and vodka. But then, one day, we decided to change our shop, and as a result, we were left with nothing but plain water.

"Uncle like Vodka...and I thought you were discussing his dog." one of Meenakshi's friends appeared out of nowhere and sat beside us, and everyone laughed. I could also see the air hostess giggling; this was becoming more like a roast than a storytelling session.

I was getting nervous, but I overlooked It. I didn't care; the urge to share my dog's story was too great.

So, that's what we did. The next decision changed our beautiful life.

"Rishi, you must come to my house today at 07:00 pm with your wife; you are invited to a small function. You see, today is my twenty-fifth wedding anniversary."

"Congratulations, Sir. I will come."

It was my boss inviting me to his house. I was still new in Haridwar, unlike my hometown, where our parents had many friends and relatives; here, I had a small circle. This was one of the first parties outside some regular office parties, so I was excited.

"Rishi sahab, do you know Sharma Sahab must be a millionaire."

My office boy Pandey whispered to me.

"Why Pandey?"

"He has a huge property right in the middle of Haridwar, at least 6,000 square feet."

"Ok, that's huge; it's like a farmhouse."

"Ohh yes, sir, huge garden with so many litchi and mango trees; he doesn't need to go for any walks outside; his campus is so big a few rounds, and he could easily complete his ten thousand steps."

"Ohh, that's the secret of his health," I laughed. My boss was a big man; he loved sweet stuff. And yes, tea, at least seven cups in a day. But he also had a big heart and was one of the coolest people I have ever worked with.

As Pandey had described, his house was like a farmhouse, the likes of which you see in the movies. His father, a civil servant in his time, apparently made this in the 50s. It had a big garden with lots of flowers and fruit trees. And it was surrounded by two big apartments. It was like a paradise amid a bustling city.

Now, as a parent, you always think about your Kid. The same is true for pet parents, too. So the first thing that came to our mind as we entered that big house was, "If we could live here or any place like it, Chuggi would love it." He could run here and there, and finally, that dog could use his guard skills properly.

I just thought it, and bloody hell, the transfers came out the following day, and he got transferred. And by the way, who did he ask to come and live in his house on rent? Hmm me!

It's said you should always be careful about what you wish for. The universe is like a genie who hears and makes your wishes come true. That day, the universe was listening to us. It whooshed its wand and said, "Your wish is my command. Let it be true!"

Damm, the universe! When you want a thing desperately, it will never give you (like that dream job where I will earn millions without doing any work and just watching Netflix the whole day). But it grants such trivial wishes that are irrelevant.

My wife also started to work, and we could afford a big house like that on rent. We saw the house again in the morning, and the same thought ran through her head: "Ohh, Chuggi would love here. The place is so huge he can practically poop anywhere he likes."

As parents, we often do things for our children out of love, which may not always be the best decision in hindsight. Most of the time, we don't consult with our children and assume we know what's best for them. This is especially true for pet parents who, by the way, cannot ask their furry friends for their opinion.

Well, but only if we could have asked Chuggi.

"Hooman, wait!"

"Sniff sniff house dangerous cats more cat."

"Sniff another dog's poop, big dog"

"Sniff Sniff backyard big lots of smell."

"Sniff, Sniff, a stranger coming and going."

"Hooman, don't be stupid! Old house best! Lots of babes. Miss them."

"And Sniff Sniff neighbour bad!"

Six

THE NIGHT WATCHMAN

"Shall I get you a coffee before you depart or leave after getting bored, and our beautiful meeting ends here?" Aditya interrupted me, looking at Meenakshi.

Boy, this story is going much faster than mine, or maybe this generation is faster. The boy has guts. In a few minutes, he is asking a girl for coffee.

"One for me, too," I said with a sarcastic smile and continued.

"Son, see, the house is big, and there are just you two," My father-in-law said.

He is a good man in his 70s who loves his walks and wakes up at 4 am, goes out daily for his walk, does yoga, and eats no sugar or salt. The guy has zero bad habits;

even at this age, he loves learning and studying astrology. The guy is a Saint! Love him

"But we have Chuggi." I looked at my dog, who was licking his rear and balls.

"Yes, he can protect you, but still, it's impractical; this house is better."

"Yes, and even the approach road is bad," said my wife.

I looked at her and wondered how quickly she had changed the party. I had already given my word to my boss, so there was no going back now.

"But Chuggi will run freely."

Her eyes sparkled again.

"I am telling you, family safety and security come first. You are now living in a beautiful apartment. Don't leave it." My father-in-law gave me this golden advice.

"Hmm," I said. But I was thinking, heck no, I don't care about any advice. I am my own man and would instead fall and break my teeth, knees, and back rather than take advice from an older man. What did he know? We had Chuggi. He could take two or three robbers down in just a jump.

Love can make us do stupid stuff, and love for kids makes us even more stupid. So stupid that we can't even think. This house change was going to be a big lesson for me.

Within a week, we would finish all the formalities. We booked our packers. The packers and movers came. Seeing them pack our whole house into small, neat boxes was so much fun. I was relieved I would finally leave this dreaded colony. My house was near my office, so even on holidays when my bosses came to the office (as they never liked to be at their homes), they called me to the office just for some tea or the routine office talk, sometimes even late in the evening.

One of them was having an affair with another employee. She used to come late in the evening on Saturdays. It was a site office, and only a few people were posted there. Hence, he kept me as a backup in case his wife appeared. Previously, he was in a relationship with a nurse who also used to visit him in the office; one day, his wife thought, How did this lousy person start working so much and decided to give him a surprise visit and caught him, a lot of commotion followed, he vowed never to do that again. Still, a month later he started goofing around with another woman. But now he took precautions. I was a junior employee, so I had to comply. Strangely, his wife also took my number and told me not to tell him and inform her about his mischief. I felt morally obliged to tell her, but I also had no intention of losing my job, so I just overlooked everything, but it cost me my Saturdays.

Also, the house here was ancient. Comparatively, my boss's house was new and good. We would have a big garden to chill in; his compound even had a badminton court.

This was going to be one of the turning points in our lives.

Who knows what we do, why we do it, why we get what we don't want and why we go where we don't want to go?

"Uncle, what a line; it's Instagram-worthy." that annoying Meenakshi friend intervened again. "And by the way, I am leaving; I don't want to get bored any more, and my flight is also here."

"Bye, take care, sweetheart."

I was happy that she left.

"However, she is right; I think I got carried away.". I said.

The air hostess turned towards us and said, "I also have a pet at home ."

"Me too had one, but she died," Aditya said.

"I am sorry." She said sympathetically.

"Yes, it happened a year ago," Aditya said, trying to score some sympathy points.

Focus, dude, I thought, but I couldn't blame him; it was the first time for me an air hostess was talking about something other than "Anything else, sir or please read the safety instructions kept in your front seat pocket, or straighten up the seats for the take-off."

"And when will this plane to Mumbai take off, madam?" Meenakshi added with a sarcastic tone

Is something happening here, or is it just my uncle's brain? No, I am not that old; why care?

"I don't know; I am on the plane to Chennai."

Her reply brought me back from those stupid thoughts; I looked towards Meenakshi with a question: Shall I continue?

"Yes, please", she replied with a smile.

The three of us sat in our car with some remaining stuff and left the old colony towards our new home with new aspirations; just about two hundred meters from the house, a veil lifted from our eyes, and we realised what we had done.

"Ohh, my God, the road here sucks !! I told you, Rishi, we shouldn't have come here."

"See, our car is being so jumpy... Look at Chuggi; he is so afraid! Now, every day, we would have to use this road, oh no. Papa was right."

"I told you, but you never listen to me." She added.

"Hey, you also liked the garden, didn't you?" I added, "And the kitchen is also big".

"No, Rishi, I have a bad feeling about this."

And then we entered the compound; it was already dark, and we realised this place was huge. It would be better with a big family and not for a small family like ours; it was a security nightmare.

"I do not like this place." She said, "Forget the garden; it's a jungle out here. There may be snakes, frogs, and God knows what else."

My wife was rightfully angry. I had seen the house in the morning, including the front garden; I had conveniently avoided the back yard, which was huge, double what was in front, apart from the fact that the approach road sucked. The house had one entrance from the main street and went through the neighbour's complex. This neighbour was my boss's relative. The whole property was shaped like a big L and sandwiched on three sides. As our house was behind their house, to approach it, we had to go through their property, and these neighbours were what to say, just not at all friendly; we didn't think about issues like at what times the gate would be locked, there was no guard anything. On top of that, every morning and evening, Chuggi must go out for his business. And through their compound.

We settled in for the night, but Chuggi was fully alert; he just sat in front of the window looking out. After all, his house has changed. His place was gone suddenly; he had a huge responsibility, a big house. And many cats were living around the compound. My dog is not a big fan of cats; he just hates them.

I think I should also tell the position of my house from my Dog's perspective.

"New house, sniff new smell, it smells pungent, hate it."

"Hooman stupid to come here."

"New house... big got to protect! Cats hate cats!"

"New house, no sleep, have to protect hoomans!!"

He wouldn't sleep at night and always be on guard like a watchman; every time we would wake up in the middle of the night, we would see him sitting by the window looking outside the backyard. It was straight from horror movies.

The backyard was so big that we started to feel the itch. Dogs have a sense; he was giving us signs about what was to happen, and his reading of the houses has always been spot-on! And he didn't like this one—especially the neighbours.

Seven

MEETING THE NEIGHBOURS.

Before coming here, I thought I would leave Chuggi out in the garden every morning without a leash, and there would be no need to take him for walks. But the following morning, I realised that even this wasn't possible. As the campuses were not segregated, if I left Chuggi, he would run around sniffing on the campus, marking his territory, going to the neighbour's area, and God forbid he would bite somebody. So I decided he couldn't run free here, and we would have to take him out from the main door for his routine walk; however, as the entrance was the same, I had to take him through our neighbour's campus.

Another thing I overlooked was that the neighbours also had a dog, an old golden retriever. My boss mentioned it, but I didn't pay much attention.

"Hello, Good Morning." I greeted them

"Hmm. Is this your dog?"

What sort of stupid question is this? Whose dog will I take for a walk? And he asked with scorn on his face like, ehh why are you here?

"Yes, he is our dog. His name is Chuggi." I replied.

"He looks dangerous. Does he bite?"

Of course he does, I thought, "Hmm, he is not that friendly."

He glared from his specs, said Hmm again, and kept watering his plants.

And then suddenly, out of nowhere, his Labrador came out and stood in front of Chuggi.

And boy, my dog barked like he would break his chain and run away now. This dog was a beautiful golden retriever, nearly 15 years old, with white furs.

Initially, he looked at him with dismay. He wasn't used to this behaviour, and he got so scared that he got fits, started shaking, and just sat on the floor and then refused to come up; it was a sorrowful sight.

Instead of helping his poor dog, the neighbour kept glaring at me while I was frantically trying to control Chuggi.

"Take your dog out, " he said angrily, and I pulled my dog outside. It seems our first meeting was just not neighbourly.

And then it also rained last night, so the bad road outside turned into a puddle. There was traffic and mud, and all the neighbouring street dogs came and they started barking at Chuggi; he also barked. I even slipped once. And even after one hour of walking, he didn't poop.

On my way back, I again saw the neighbour; this time, his wife was also there with the poor dog still lying on the ground.

I looked at them with a sorry expression, and they glared back at me like I was some criminal. I didn't say anything and walked straight home feeling irritated.

"Let's go and meet them". My wife suggested, "It would also cool things down."

"Ehh, I don't want to go; I don't like them; I don't think it will do any good."

"No, silly, let's go; they are our neighbours; we must be good with them".

Somehow, my wife persuaded me, and we met them at their house to clear some air and create goodwill.

"Hello, how are you? We have just shifted here," My wife said to them.

The lady looked at us from top to bottom and said, "Yes, please come in; I am Namita."

"I am Radhika, and this is Rishi; he is in the same office as your brother." My wife said.

"Ohh yes, Cheeku told me about you; that's his childhood name." I thought that was an interesting name, although now he looks more like a watermelon. Again, who am I to judge when I myself was turning into a cantaloupe?

"So, do you like it here?" She asked.

"Yes, the property is so big, just like a house in the 70s; who can afford such a house these days? But yes, probably we will take some time to adjust."

"Yes, don't worry, and we are here too."

She seemed nice, I thought to myself. My wife looked at me with a smile. And then she added.

"You have a dog. He looks aggressive. What's his name?"

"Chuggi, and yes, he is a bit aggressive. You also have a dog, I suppose. I am sorry for today. Chuggi gets very aggressive when he sees another dog."

"Okay, keep him away from our baby. His name is Tommy, and he is 15 years old. He is still in shock, and I had to take him to the doctor after that incident. And you know the total expense was Rs 5000; who will give that money?" she said. My wife and I looked at each other in shock; this conversation quickly taken such a wrong turn. And that's not the way to greet your neighbours.

"Well, our dog didn't harm him, and dogs bark at each other, especially male dogs." I felt my temper rising. Who says such a thing? They still haven't offered us a glass of water and are asking for money straight away.

My wife held my hand, signalling to calm down.

"Yes, actually, he is very aggressive. That's why you see we are planning to install one gate so that he might not run away accidentally and do any harm, and anyway, one of our major reasons for shifting here was that our dog can have some free space to run around."

"No, how can you install a gate? I will talk to Cheeku about it." Namita said.

"Maam, why are you getting hyper? We just..."

The gate touched some nerves. The property was evenly divided between my boss and his sister; however, the passage was still not decided, so there was some tension, and our gate installation signalled to them that their property would be divided.

"No, you cannot do this." The husband said.

"Our dog will also come every evening to your campus to relieve himself; he always used to come when Cheeku was living there."

"We are paying rent, and our dog is there. We will not be responsible if anything happens to you or your dog inside that campus. Rishi, let's go," my wife replied angrily. And now this will be trespassing, and this is not your campus where you can take your dog for a walk."

And we stormed out. Thinking, what the hell was that all about? This was some crazy-level shit.

We talked with my boss, and he assured us that he would talk with them, and after that, we also didn't care much. We minded our own business, and they theirs. We installed the gate as said. Initially, we loved it there. A big Garden and lots of places for my dog to run, but still, he wasn't that happy because he probably got a whiff or a smell of the future in that house.

As the main problem was still there. Our gate was a problem for them. They objected and said you wouldn't lock it. My boss asked us to cooperate as they used to this routine for a long time; we agreed but warned him of the consequences if Chuggi was free. But still, their dog kept coming, especially when we were outside, whereas I was taking Chuggi outside the campus for his walks.

For Chuggi, a stranger dog peeing and pooping in his territory is a big no. He used to bark his heart out, but they didn't care.

We tried to reason with them, but they saw us as property claimants. Even after our repeated warnings, they continued their routine behind our backs.

Now every dog owner knows this, especially if you own a rowdy and hot head dog like ours; know that shit may happen anytime, and you must always be alert.

"Let me get some coffee; I am still feeling a bit sleepy; getting up at 04:00 am to take a flight at 09:00 am."

"Please continue; you are not coming to the main point and simply beating around the bush.", Meenakshi said angrily.

"You should go to the second counter there; he makes superb coffee." The air hostess also added.

Today was my lucky day; an air hostess sat near me and was now talking to me and giving suggestions, too.

"You should be coming here regularly?" Aditya asked

" Yes, I am an air hostess after all, and I am posted here these days."

"Hi, I am Rishi. I am going to Mumbai. Where are you from?" I asked, forgetting about my coffee.

"I am Shivani from Gwalior. And by the way, I also want a coffee. Shall I accompany you there?"

"Ahmm Ahmm", I coughed. "Sure, why not? Gwalior is such a beautiful city; we visited it once; let's get that coffee."

And God knows from where that annoying Meenakshi friend appeared and brought us five coffees.

"There is no need to go anywhere; if you don't mind, I ordered the coffee, and it's on me. Something's about to happen, and I can feel it. And also, you are not coming to the point."

"Your flight?"

"The boarding is yet to start; please continue, uncle." She said with an evil smile.

Chuggi was feeling the tension. He was always on alert on that campus. He usually sleeps a lot, like eighteen hours a day, but here he was, always awake, looking out; A lot was going on in his mind.

"Boww bow bow I hate that dog..."

"Bowww.... So many cats here and another dog's poop.."

"Grrrr.... How you peee..........Grrr ...Will see you..."

"Grrr human useless.... Will take the matter in my paw..."

"Just ... this door.... Grrrr...."

This peace didn't last long; there were routine, uncomfortable exchanges. Her husband even once threatened to kill Chuggi.

We were now getting irritated, but we kept our calm. It came to an extent when my boss's wife said not to extend the lease of the house beyond one year. We also decided it's enough; now it's time to shift.

But before we could move out, Chuggi finally got a chance to take matters into his hand or paw. On one fine Sunday, we planned to visit the local National Park. As usual, Chuggi was anxious. He doesn't like us going out on weekends, and as soon as he saw my DSLR bag, his anxiety increased, and he barked his heart out. But we still went there. We got a bit late while returning in the evening. As our car entered, we could hear Chuggi barking loudly, but this was not an anxious bark but a warning bark. As soon we reached the gate, he sensed us and started barking anxiously, so we didn't give it so much notice. I quickly opened the gate, closed back the gate we installed, and left him unleashed outside to run around the campus before I could take him for his walk.

When the gate opened, he ran like a rocket straight towards the backyard. The neighbour's husband was there with their dog. Even after we repeatedly said no, they came to our campus. Chuggi grabbed the poor golden retriever's tail; I tried to stop him, but no. It was a gruesome fight; he paused for a while, and I pulled him by his collar. The rest may be summarised as follows: The poor golden retriever was admitted. He somehow survived.

"Your dog is so bad. Our baby is hurt so much. Take him away, or we will kill him." The husband came the next day and threatened us.

"How dare you threaten us like that. It wasn't his fault. We are paying rent for this property, and you trespassed here without our permission. And if you even try harming the dog, we will complain to the police about this trespassing." I retorted.

That night, we had a long discussion with my boss and decided it was time to change this house, so we increased our search for our new home.

If Chuggi could have shared his opinion, he would have said

"Grrrr, bad hoomans , I told you so."

"My place, My home. Why did this dog come?"

"Go away. My home Go away..."

"Big house, lots of cats. Security breach. Protect my hooman protect my family."

Interestingly, I never complained about what happened. It was, after all, their fault. We had warned them many times. Their dog once had fits seeing Chuggi bark.

But you see, the underline problem was not with them; this heroic attitude of my dog was going to bite me in the ass.

"That's why you should get a dog. It was just not his fault. Your dog did good." Meenakshi said

"Yes, we had a Labrador at home when I was about ten. He used to do nothing, sit and eat, and he got obese; we used to say joyfully he would be friends with the thieves. My dad would have loved Chuggi. It's his duty, and he did it. Why do you have an issue? Shivani said.

"You see, it's not about biting but how he jumped on the other dog. It was in our residential campus, but the result would be the same even if it were outside the campus."

"It's just not his fault," Meenakshi said.

Yes, they were right. Even Chuggi was right, but still, I wish he was more like a Labrador; probably, I didn't deserve such a strong-willed guard dog.

My thoughts went back to a year ago....

"I think we should change this home," I said to my wife

"What, you are nuts! You should throw this dog out. I am scared. That lady had no fault. I saw what he did. She was bleeding badly Rishi. And you want us to move."

"No, not for that reason; your office will be nearer. And I am also thinking of doing something about this dog."

I knew I had no idea. He had bit my maid, and that's too unprovoked. Changing the house was probably my exit strategy in this 'Fight or Flight situation' I chose 'Flight'. I didn't know what to do. I was scared that she might make a police complaint. Or maybe my neighbours might do something to my dog.

My father-in-law shared a video on WhatsApp showing a dog mauled a small kid. It scared the shit out of me. Because I have seen my dog biting and knew what he could do, whenever he used to growl on my neighbour's Kid that's too unprovoked, it sends shivers down my spine. I know what he is capable of! My mom called me and told me that this dog needed to be euthanised or sent off somewhere.

A dog's behaviour becomes bad/aggressive or unacceptable to us humans, primarily because of the inability of his owner to train him. And an aggressive, willed solid cocky dog like Chuggi needs proper training and socialising. Train him? We didn't have time to spend or play with him; we left him alone every day for long hours. Socialising him was out of the question. In India, you even don't have a proper place to walk your dog. Almost all of our houses to date have been in the heart of the city around a bustling marketplace. Now, there are people, cars and other dogs. Every day is a challenge to walk him.

Killing this dog would be like killing one of my family members, leaving him someplace I know his sense of smell he would come running back to us to leave him in an animal shelter is our best option, but he is only seven years old and still in the best of his health. He would miss us and wait for us for the rest of his life. I would miss him. He is one of the most essential parts of our lives. He is our happiness; he is home.

"Hey, are you there?" Meenakshi said.

"Hmm, never mind, I just got carried away, all the memories and everything," I said.

"Your dog did good. It's not his fault". Shivani said.

"This was the start of his violent streak or biting streak. On the same campus. The neighbour Gardner, who came inside without our knowledge, got bitten."

"But we didn't care because, as you said, we also felt it wasn't his fault then. We had found a new house and were ready to move again."

Eight

NEW HOUSE. NEW SMELLS.

Within a week, we found a new house. Haridwar is a small city, and it's easy to find homes for rent, and the rent is also not that high. And so we shifted again. Shifting is always a big headache, changing addresses and taking everything from one place to another. I blamed my dog for it. After all, if he hadn't bitten people, we would still be living there. But yes, we were relieved, too. The place was too big for a small family.

The new house was smaller and nearer to my office. As soon as we arrived at the new place, Chuggi ran inside the house and started doing zoomies in the garden. This time Chuggi was very much at home! He surveyed the whole house, all the rooms and even the terrace, barked at the neighbours next door, and then peacefully settled in the garden at the front. He was happy and content. He gave the security check to that place with the expression that this much area he could protect.

The house was still big but not that big, with a small yet decent-sized garden and ample space to park my vehicle in the backyard. It was perfect. My current landlord was staying in Baroda, and there were no relatives as neighbours. His only condition was that the rent be paid on time. For the rest, he didn't care.

We loved this new house with its small lawn in front. Chuggi ran around the house, hunted rats, and was happy. My office was nearer, and my wife's office was also not that far. The neighbours didn't care about us, and we didn't care about them.

However, having a dog like Chuggi will always present some challenges.

Like, every morning, we used to meet two dogs walking off-leash. They were trained and usually didn't disturb other dogs and people, but Chuggi would bark at them as soon as they came under his radar. They retaliated by barking at him, and since they were off-leash, they could go very close to him, and there would be a bow-bow fest. I tried to reason with the owner to put his dogs on leash, but he didn't listen. Then, one day, Chuggi took matters into his own hands when his leash slipped from my hand, and he caught one of the dogs by its tail. When the other dog came to rescue, Chuggi jumped on him, too ,biting off his ear. Their owner finally understood, and I never saw them on that route again.

But still, there were others, like , a male adolescent dog got impressed by Chuggi's aggressive skills and would follow us and do belly rolls on the ground to get his attention; my dog would still bark at him, but he wouldn't listen and still wanted to make Chuggi his master so he continued to follow us, and it irritated me because Chuggi would pull me and bark his heart out at the dog.

In addition, there were many other pet dogs in that locality, and every dog owner used to take their dog to the same park; there was one female Dalmatian who lived in the back lane, three Labradors living not that far and who used to go out for walks together every day, one German shepherd living two houses away, and two other pooches who also used to walk off-leash. And all of them would come in the way of Chuggi's walk.

The real challenge was taking him for walks in the evening, especially after it got dark. I would pray that there wouldn't be any dogs or, worse, cats combined with a human walking carelessly in our path, and always had to be on full alert mode.

All this gave me a headache, but still, this house was perfect, with its lovely garden and a big terrace where you can sit and enjoy the sun in the winter.

And except for the issues with his walks, Chuggi has a lot of lovable quirks. For example, he will disturb me only when I am in a good mood. He will only want to go out then and play with me if I sit and do my office work. He never disturbs me, but as soon as I take out my book or watch a movie on the same laptop, He knows that I am relaxed, and his paw would be on my lap, indicating that he wants to go out or would like to play. He starts running and doing Zoomies with my socks or some used plastic in his mouth! He waits for us all day and sleeps during that time as we are both in the office. After dinner, he becomes active, barks, asks for his treats and runs here and there. If my wife encounters a cockroach or lizard and screams, he rushes to her aid and attempts to locate the insect. If it approaches Chuggi, it is promptly eliminated.

Sitting outside by the bonfire with my furry friend Chuggi on chilly winter nights was amazing. He's not afraid of the fire but can't stand the smoke. He gets terrified when he's exposed to vehicle exhaust smoke. When he was a puppy, his nose got too close to a Bullet motorcycle's silencer, and just at that moment, the driver started the bike, which traumatised him. Now, whenever he sees any motorcycle or car exhaust while walking, he either jumps to the side or stops in his tracks.

"Hearing all this makes me want to have a dog now," Meenakshi said

"I wish all the days could be the same."

Eleven Months ago

"Leave him now! He is just an animal; leave him. Doesn't your kid matter to you?" My mother called me on the phone, sounding both worried and angry.

"My Grand Kid means everything to me. I want you to leave him now!"

"Yes, Maa, working on it," I said in a heavy voice.

So much has changed. How did Chuggi go from being the apple of our eye to this?

Nine

THE ROOF

"You seem to be lost again?" Meenakshi said.

"Yes, as I said earlier some happy memories, some sad ones," I said.

"Okay, but still, it doesn't seem that bad; all you have to do is take your dog for a walk and just find a place and leave him."

"Ask any dog owner; there is a reason why leaving your dog at dog boarding facilities is a big problem, at least it is for me. Firstly, finding a proper place is a challenge. Then, when you leave him at a dog boarding facility, it's like you left him randomly, and now you are gone forever, and he will wait for you every minute. Also, not many places keep the dogs well; they will be kept in a cage or chained the whole day. Sometimes, they won't take him for a walk, so he pees there where he is chained and gets beaten for too

much barking. The dogs are not free. Also, they don't chain him properly, the leash would be too tight for any movement, and he would sit all day, unable to lie down. And all of this while you would be chilling out somewhere."

"As for walking, yes, it is good and can be a very rewarding experience too. But there will be days when you don't want to go out. But you can't say no to it. You will have to go out in the morning and evening every day till he is alive; there is just no way you can avoid it. And if you have a male, then during mating season, he won't sleep and would cry and wake up at odd hours. It takes a lot of patience to be with a dog." I said with a sigh.

"My boyfriend wants a dog, but I am not ready to take our relationship to that level. And now, hearing you, my apprehensions have increased. As a kid, I had a dog at home, a beautiful Golden retriever; he was so friendly and was always happy. He used to even sleep on my bed. His name was Coco, and we loved him. But my father handled all these issues of taking him to the doctor or taking him for a walk. Also, someone was always at home, and the house was big, too. Therefore, we never gave much thought to these issues," The air hostess added.

"Yes, that was my point, too; previously, dogs were usually kept in big houses in the cities or with farmers in villages to look after their farm animals, where there was space to run and more people who could handle them; now we live alone in apartments the dog can't go out on his own, he is dependent on you for his walks and exercise. You have to take responsibility for his walks, health, and

everything, and most people cannot afford a full-time dog attendant."

After this long monologue, everyone went silent. Aditya was strangely quiet during this discussion and seemed to be in his own thoughts.

"Hmm, it seems this flight will take forever to take off," I said, trying to break the eerie silence.

"Well, you are an air hostess. Do you like waiting at airports?" I asked, trying to change the topic.

"It's my job, and that's what I have signed up for; also, it's fun talking to passengers, meeting new people, and talking to random strangers about anything other than their safety briefing, which no one cares about," she said with a smile.

"Still waiting at an airport for me is like you're all dressed up in your uniform, ready to take on the day. You arrive at the airport bright and early and make your way to the crew room, where you're met with a group of tired-looking flight attendants who are all trying to wake up with their morning coffee."

"You exchange some witty banter and maybe even share some hilarious stories from previous flights. But just as you're getting into the groove of things, your captain barges in with a mountain of paperwork needed before the flight can take off."

"So, you put on your game face and get to work, but not before making a few jokes about how you'll need more caffeine to make it through the day. As the passengers start to arrive, you're stationed at the gate, where you're met

with a mixture of excited vacationers and grumpy business travellers."

"But you're a pro at this, so you take it all in stride, cracking some jokes and doing your best to keep everyone happy. And just when you think you're in the clear, you hear the dreaded announcement: 'Attention all passengers, we regret to inform you that your flight has been delayed...' just like today."

"Cue the groans and eye rolls from the passengers, but you and your fellow flight attendants take it in stride, making silly faces and cracking jokes to lighten the mood. And when the flight finally takes off, you can't help but breathe a sigh of relief and share a laugh with your colleagues, knowing that you've successfully navigated another day in the life of an air hostess."

"Cool," said Aditya.

"That's a lot about me; please, I want to hear more about your story. It's important for me, too; my relationship kind of depends on it, although it's not the only issue we disagree on. Lately, we have been fighting quite often; I don't know, but maybe getting a dog might help." She said.

I will again resume with his walks. This is the only time he gets the most action in his life. There are issues, but looking at the half-full side of the glass, one of the best things about having a dog is waking up early, taking them for a walk, and enjoying the morning. However, having a dog is like having a mandatory morning alarm clock with no snooze button. Occasionally, you may get lucky, and they might go back to sleep, but they will always return. After all, when you got to go, you got to go.

A dog can wake you up in many ways, such as licking you or barking. Chuggi has a unique way of waking me up.

"Is this important?" Aditya intervened.

"Shh, let him continue", Meenakshi corrected him.

"He seems confused". Shivani added, " Just now, he gave that long monologue about why not to take the dog for a walk."

"Yes, the whole life is one big confusion about what's right and what's wrong. Nothing is fully right or wrong. Yes, I am confused, and hopefully, you might get some clarity from my confusion."

Firstly, he will use his nose: A healthy dog's nose is always wet, but when it touches you on a cold winter morning, it's like someone has kept a cold, damp sponge on your feet. It signals that he has woken up and wants to go out and pee. But as it's a gentle push, I know he can control his pee at this stage. So I pretend not to wake up and stay still on the bed. In the mornings, we usually want to go to the bathroom when we wake up. Me getting up from bed would signal to Chuggi that I am awake and am ready to take him out, and then in the excitement, he develops a pressure like he will poop here only and will start to bark loudly. So I control my urges and roll over to the other side or pretend to lie still; going to the bathroom can wait a few more minutes.

SECOND comes to the paw:- Now, after five odd minutes, Chuggi places both his paws on the bed and tries to tap my face with his one paw; it sounds so cute, right? But it's not; firstly, the dog's paws are rough, and I never did any nail trimming (frankly, I was scared of him, and we thought, why disturb the natural order). Secondly, I know the places where he pees and poops. And they are not the cleanest places on Earth. Additionally, he will pee where the other dogs have done their business. So grudgingly, I have to wake up.

But I have one more snooze button for this doggy Alarm.

THIRD.:- The last weapon in my arsenal is this line: " Chuggi, it's still night, go back to sleep". And 80 out of 100 times, he obeys and goes back to sleep; this is the only trick we could ever teach him.

FOURTH- Well, the doggy found a way to avoid my snoozing. One day, while I was on a tour, my father-in-law came to Haridwar to care for my wife. Now he had to take him on the walk, and he took him to walk at 04:00 am, and he didn't snooze Chuggi. Chuggi loved that, and he knew he also had another option, so whenever my father-in-law was in the house, Chuggi would go and put his paw on his bed and get his walk at 04:00 am.

"How is all of this data relevant to your story?" Aditya interrupted again.

"Please let me continue. If you don't want to know, you can leave." I said angrily

"Chill, dude," he said.

"Okay, so where was I?"

"Somewhere around, how does your dog wake you up? "Meenakshi said.

All this waking up early led us to take morning walks. During one of my wife's morning walks, something happened that I want to mention.

"Ohh, so that's why the build-up", Aditya said smilingly.

I wasn't at home that day. My wife went on her walk alone, and she thought Instead of leaving Chuggi, in the garden, she could leave him on the terrace because there was more space for him to run around. As Chuggi was used to being on a balcony, she was confident he would not jump off the terrace.

While my wife was still walking, our neighbour called and asked her to return immediately. It was something regarding our dog being trapped on the terrace.

There was bitch in that locality; she was usually shy and sometimes would follow us but from a safe distance, usually during our morning walks. But during mating season, she started coming to our gate. But she wasn't alone; three male dogs who were after her would also follow her. Chuggi would bark madly at them, so after a few days, we shooed her away. And she didn't return after that, so we didn't give that incident much importance.

On that day, she returned with her suitors; all she wanted was Chuggi. Unfortunately, my boy wasn't in the Garden. If he had been there, he would have jumped the fence and taken care of the other three dogs to be united in the great pleasure of Nature. But he was one floor above.

Seeing her and the other dogs, a mixture of anger and arousal arose in him. Overpowered by these emotions, he jumped over the terrace. Luckily, there was a parapet, and he landed on it—a paw here or there, and he would have fallen by a height of Fifteen feet to the ground. He kept standing still at that location with his ears to the side and tail between his legs, but being him, he continued barking at the other dogs.

Neighbours gathered at the sight. Something interesting happened in that dull society, and somebody even called a fire truck.

When my wife returned running, she saw Chuggi stranded, looking scared, and a fire truck parked in front of our house.

The fireman saw my wife. She said he was very sleepy and looked like he didn't know what to do. Typically, not many such incidents of pets being trapped at a height happen in Haridwar. Even if they do, no one calls the firemen. It was their first chance to do something like this.

As he was preparing to place the ladder and was waiting for his hero moment, some young girls in their pyjamas were also out with their phones ready for their Instagram story; my wife was trying to reason with him to let her go up that ladder the distance was not that much, and the dog is aggressive. Both his ears were down to the side then, so he seemed nervous and harmless.

The fireman said, "No, ma'am, I will do it; I have a German shepherd at home, too." And he placed the stairs

As soon as he was face to face with this thick-headed dog, Chuggi snarled at him, showing his big canines, and barked so loudly that the poor guy fell with his ladder.

"I told you so," she said.

Ultimately, she used the same stairs, picked him up with one hand, and brought him down.

And as soon as he was down, he started barking at everyone again.

"I think you are making it up," said Shivani.

"No, it's a true story," I said

"Aditya, what do you think?" Meenakshi asked

"How could you leave your dog unsupervised and unprotected? He could have got badly hurt or worse. Aditya said all this in a very loud tone.

"Firstly, it was our terrace, and there were no prior incidents. Why are you getting angry? He was fine. And such incidents can happen."

"People are very careless with their dogs. They just leave them like they are some things," Aditya mumbled. "I do not like your story. I am leaving."

Something touched him. We all looked at him in shock. I was getting angry. Firstly, he constantly interrupted me, and then there was this melodrama. And from my perspective, it was still a light-hearted incident. There was

no need to be this angry, " It's my story, and she wants to hear it." I said, pointing at Meenakshi. "And you are free to go."

"Dude, who are you? Why are you getting angry? We are enjoying ourselves. I want to hear his story. You can go anywhere else. It's not that I care?" Meenakshi added angrily.

What is happening here? It seemed this was the end of our small encounter. And if his melodrama continues, he will waste unnecessary time, the flight might take off, and my only chance to share my story with two beautiful ladies will disappear. I cursed him under my breath.

Aditya cooled down and looked back at Meenakshi. They kept staring for ten seconds, and no one spoke. All this was too filmy. Could his cringy lines have this effect on a girl? On top of this, these two were smiling at each other in between. Meenakshi was tucking her hair behind her ears. It seemed love at first sight for these kids; aww, young love. Or this is my uncle's brain's imagination again.

This dude was not going anywhere.

"Ok, Bye then, but one thing, why this sour face, Aditya? Did I say something hurtful? "I said to break that awkward silence.

"Something like that happened with me, too."

"It's about your dog?" Meenakshi asked

"No sweety's."

"Now, who is this sweety?" Shivani asked.

"Sweety?? Your sister?" Meenakshi asked, raising her eyebrow.

"Shall I continue my story? I think our aeroplane is also about to take off."

"No, a long-lost old acquaintance," said Aditya.

Ten

THE PREGNANCY

Aditya seemed to be lost in his thoughts. I looked at him and decided his sadness wasn't worth stopping my story.

I looked at Meenakshi. She seemed a bit sad, too. Her sadness was much worth it to my boy's brain. It cannot remain idle when it sees a beautiful, sad girl and wants to rush to console her. I signalled Aditya to sit back. And he sat down grudgingly.

" So shall I continue."

"Ok". Aditya and Meenakshi said together.

" Well, I think we should try for a baby?"

"Hmm, ok." The thought was exciting and scary. But at that moment, I couldn't say no to my wife. After all, it's the main reason you get married, apart from that our careers were also settled. So, there was no reason for me to say no. But still, I was scared.

Anyhow, my fears gave way to passion.

My friend in the HR department (whom we nicknamed HR) had a Kid recently. It was so good to see him with his boy.

"You know half my salary goes where?" He asked me one day

"Your salary, your house, I don't care" I shrugged

"Diapers." Apparently, he also didn't care whether I was listening.

But seeing him running here and there for errands made me wonder, do I want a kid right now? After all, I can't care for myself; how will I care for a baby?

"Every man is scared of commitment," Shivani said sarcastically. "First, they don't want to commit, then they don't want to marry, and you didn't want to have kids. All men are the same."

"Honestly, that wasn't the thing I was scared of."

"The real reason was my darling Chuggi."

When I saw my friend's kid running here and there in the house and all his toys on the floor, I realised my dog does the same in my house: a shoe here, a piece of torn paper and lots and lots of hair everywhere. Chuggi has wavy brown hair with a white tip. How would my child run here and there with this scary dog?

The other thing was that this dog was never socialised, and his circle was very small, including only our parents and siblings.

And he isn't that big of a fan of kids.

I couldn't say this to anyone. My fears were there. Alone, I was seeing videos on YouTube about "How to raise dogs and kids together." If I had said this to my parents or any friend, the only answer would have been to leave this dog. And I loved him too much; I couldn't do that to him.

"Baby, it has not come", my wife smiled after one month of our trying period.

My eyes widened; I knew what she meant. She had missed her period. I ran to buy the pregnancy kit.

"Does this count? One dark and one faint line?" she was smiling. The test result was out, and we were expecting a baby!

It's an extraordinary feeling when you realise you will be a Dad; I was still in shock, trying to figure out what happened.

You see, we all have a bit of Drishyam Ajay Devgan in us, and as soon as I heard I was going to be a father, my fatherly instincts fired up. I was looking at various problematic scenarios, particularly the ones involving my dog.

Firstly, I knew he wasn't like those friendly dogs you see on those YouTube videos with babies. He is an alpha male, and that has its risk. Then, both of us are working;

how would we manage a baby? Also, getting a Nanny was out of the question because this dog doesn't like any outsider, and God forbid the worst may happen.

Life is filled with so many ifs and buts. We are constantly walking on a tightrope, but somehow we manage.

So yes, she was pregnant. I told all my friends and our family members that we were so excited when those trips to the doctor's clinic started. I bought Mother's Horlicks for her. She started caring for her health, making a hearty breakfast, and carrying protein-rich snacks. Chuggi was still well, licking his balls, cleaning his rear, and always looking for other male dogs barking and running in the house.

My mom complained about the dog shedding hair and having dirty feet, which affects hygiene, especially with the baby around.

"Hmm, you should seriously think about this dog; he is a good dog, but we should take all the necessary precautions with a baby on the way." Her father cautioned.

"My grandchild is coming, and after a long time (it was only three years), we hear good news. Nothing should happen to my grandchild; he might be a kid for you, but he is the light of our families. I am telling you to get rid of the dog." Her mother was frantic.

"Hmm, I will think about it" was my reply.

Frankly, we had no plans; we were also worried, but our love for Chuggi was still too much.

As the pregnancy progressed, so did the joys and worries. We were still in the first trimester; my father-in-law planned to visit Haridwar with his brother.

Winter had come to Haridwar. The jackets and mufflers were out, and it was cold and raining. Wrapped in their shawls and mufflers, they disembarked the train. They were like best buddies, laughing and pulling each other's legs.

Both of them are fitness freaks. While my father-in-law has a morning routine from 04:00 am to 09:00 am, which involves 7 kilometres of walking and 2 hours of yoga sessions, his big brother has the same routine with just one difference: he walks faster and does power yoga!

During those days, we played cards and did yoga, and in the evenings, we had tea and fritters with everyone in their blankets and sweaters.

And then we decided to go out to Mussoorie. And we were up for a surprise. As we started getting closer to Mussoorie, it began to rain more and then as the height increased, it started to snow! It was the first time we witnessed snowfall; it was bliss!

They returned in a few days, and it was time for the next check-up.

As my wife entered the ultrasound chamber, I sat nervously outside, looking at the poster of Lamas exercises. I took a photograph and made a mental note to ensure she did those exercises.

The doctor called me in.

"You see, there is no heartbeat. This usually happens in the first time pregnancies."

He said all this so coldly that we were both in shock; what on Earth just happened? There is no heartbeat. The medical term for this is missed abortion.

This guy hasn't even come into our world; what did we do wrong? Why did this happen?

We didn't talk to each other on our way back, and as soon as we entered home and looked at each other, tears started coming from our eyes. Crying together, we sat in the bed. Chuggi sensed something and placed his paw on my lap, and we hugged him and cried. He consoled us in his doggy way. Dogs are always there for us when we need them.

"It must have been such an emotional incident for both of you," Meenakshi said

"We would cry again, but this time it would be for him," I said, and my thoughts went back eleven months ago.

"You know na we would have to leave him". My wife was still in shock.

I looked into those brown eyes; they weren't evil, but why do you do this, Chuggi?

And so, I cried, and I cried again and again when no one was looking. This is such a special dog; he is our kid, too; he is a part of the small world that we created. He didn't ask us to pick him up; we took him in, and because of my fault, as I was too lazy to get him trained, I have to leave him now only because he is an animal and is unpredictable.

Eleven

AND LIFE GOES ON.

"It must have been hard", the air hostess said.

"Yes," I said. I looked at her badge," so you are a Kapoor, Shivani Kapoor. A heavy surname."

"Ahh, yes." She smiled. "I have such good memories of my dog; Coco loved to bath and in summers would sit in the bathroom to beat the heat, and when we installed the AC, he would not budge from the room, and God forbids if the lights went out and the Ac got switched off he would bark so loudly and would pacify only after a treat."

"Nice..." said Aditya in a very low voice, and again, he seemed lost, as though his mind was elsewhere.

"Please don't stop. Continue your story. Your boarding may start anytime soon." She said

Life went on, and for Chuggi, everything was just the same. His routine was the same. Bark for going out, Bark on other dogs, bark on humans, bark on cats, and run here and there. Always eager to eat food and always ready to play. That's his only mindset, whereas we humans change. From the optimistic and happy childhood to the cranky teenagers and then the fun-loving young adults, we get married and have kids, after that, grumpy wives and indifferent husbands. Then, we get old, sad, worried, and pathetic.

That's probably why people love their dogs much more; everyone changes except their dogs.

My cousin decided to visit us. Still in his third year, this was his first visit alone. I have seen my dog biting other people, so I was scared for him, but he was determined to befriend him; still in college, he seemed scared of nothing. So, one day, when we were out, he approached this dog and patted him. Chuggi understood this was an important person and responded well. The next thing we knew was receiving a photograph on WhatsApp of him playing with Chuggi playfully, taking his hand in his mouth! He will be the only person apart from our parents with whom this dog will ever befriend.

We were all sitting on the terrace enjoying the winter sun; it was still foggy, and we could hear bells from the nearest temple. It was Sunday, and we all enjoyed a friendly game of carrom. My wife prepared tasty biryani. Seeing the whole family together, Chuggi became very happy; the dogs picked up the vibe of the moment. So he just randomly started running and doing Zoomies. I had a newspaper in my hand, and as soon as I put that down, It was taken. And boy, he loved playing with it, thrashing it, and then he slept on the mess that he had created. We laughed, clicked some photographs and posted them on Social Media.

Then, hearing the laughter, on the opposite side of the terrace, a Dalmatian dog stood on her front paws and was looking toward us. Chuggi has developed a crush on her. With his paws on the boundary, he stood up, looked at her with his tongue out, and started cooing.

I looked into his eyes and said, "Dude, she is way beyond your league; she is a purebred. And you are a lowly mixed-breed dog. Don't even think about her."

My cousin laughed and said, "Like he can understand you, Bhaiya; their love is physical. No emotions are involved. I wish our lives were that simple, too."

Chuggi didn't sleep that night and cried, looking out our window towards her house. She was in heat, and her smell was too tempting for him.

All this crying and cooing didn't allow me to sleep, and fearing the neighbours would complain, I took him for a walk at 3:30 AM. He dragged me to her house.

Sniffing, licking any trace of her pee and then again moaning. Well, this season, he was a little bit more horny and thirsty for love. Which returns every year and takes away my sleep.

This cycle repeats everywhere and every season. But at that time, his attraction towards her was a bit too strong.

"Did Chuggi meet with her lover?" Meenakshi interrupted again.

"Let me continue my story, please. Please don't break the flow."

"Hey, who is that?" Meenakshi asked Aditya; apparently, he was staring at some photographs in his purse.

" Wait, that's your dog?" I strained my neck to look into his purse.

"Or Sweety's; why do you have so much obsession about her dog?" Meenakshi asked.

"And it looks cute, too; what's his or her name?" Shivani asked

"Well, it is a she and her name is Lucy," Aditya said.

"So, after all, who is this Sweety?" Shivani said

"Yes, tell us who this girl is. And were you two close?" Meenakshi said.

"I think let's hear from Aditya first. Chuggi's love story can wait. So, bro, would you care to shed some light on Sweety's Lucy? I want to have another coffee, maybe a cold coffee this time. It's a bit hot and crowded in here." I said.

Shivani added, "Okay, so Aditya, let's hear your version; there must be some reason this dog found a place in your purse."

"Yes," Aditya said

"Dude.. please; now you have the centre stage, let's hear from you. Don't worry, we won't judge you," I said smilingly.

Twelve

THE BEST THERAPIST HAS FURS AND FOUR LEGS.

Well, I was born and brought up here in Kolkata by my grandfather. My mother and father died in a car accident when I was very small. I loved my Grandfather very much. He owned an old house in Baghbazar, North Kolkatta; the house was big, and four families were living on rent there. Dada used to take me to school and read me stories. He was my best friend. Although I lived in a big house with many families nearby, I was a shy kid. I loved studying and being in my world playing video games.

And when I was eleven, tragedy struck me again; Dada left me one night; I still can't remember when I last felt such pain. Once again, I was left alone in this world.

I didn't know what to do; I lost all interest in studies, no one cared about me, and I cared about no one; there was one Mrs Sen; she was one of the tenants, and she took my care for about two years, and then she shifted too, after that I went on a spiral down, the school kicked me out, I got into the habit of smoking, and then someone introduced me to drugs especially Charas and then Heroin, when all the money that I collected as the rent was finished, I started selling items in the house to have more money, for drugs.

One of these days, the Chatterjees shifted near my house. Mr Chatterjee was a high-ranking government official. They were mostly reserved. But their daughter was different, playful and running around here and there.

She was like sunshine with big eyes, straight black hair, milky skin; in that neighbourhood, she was the prettiest girl.

But this story is not about her. It is about Lucy, her pet dog.

"This story seems too familiar", Shivani said thoughtfully.

"No, I am not concerned with the girl. She was way above my league. And she never even cared to look at me. It was her dog."

So as they settled, I noticed every evening Sweety would come out with her dog, and an attendant would also bc with her; she was the neighbourhood's main attraction, and boys who had nothing to do would just sit and wait for her to come out.

I would also be one of them; I had dropped out of school and lost all interest in probably everything. Sitting in the corner with my drug pouch, I would see her perfect life where everything sorted out.

Honestly, I didn't care much about Lucy; she was this big Labrador. I never had a pet and was never interested in one.

And one morning, I heard that the Chatterjees were moving; I went there to see them one last time as a part of my routine. Their truck was packed, and I saw them getting in their ambassador, but Lucy was nowhere to be seen.

At night, I heard a dog crying, and the noise was coming from outside near the Chatterjees home; I saw them leave in the morning, so why was this noise? Maybe some random dog was crying, I thought and tried to sleep again.

But there was something in that dog's voice; that pain was too similar, bringing back my pains; I couldn't sleep. So I woke from my bed and went straight to my window towards the noise. And there I saw Lucy sitting before their Gate, crying and cooing.

It seemed that they didn't take Lucy with them; they left her somewhere far off, and she came running back to the house only to find that they were gone.

I felt as if her abandonment was the same as mine; I never had a pet and had no experience with one, but I could understand her pain. And then it started to rain.

I don't know what got to me, but a deep voice inside me said, I can't let her feel the same pain; it was that nagging voice inside our head that is always telling us to do the right thing, but we keep on shushing it, well that night I felt it was too powerful, and so around midnight, I took my grandfather's big old umbrella, went towards her. She was sitting right on the road. She looked at me and waved her tail. Somehow, my presence comforted her. I took her in my umbrella, and she rubbed her back against my legs; her wet hair brushed me at that moment; I felt like some higher power was telling me to take her home. I believed my grandfather sent her to me that night; I had brought one chapatti with me; I called her near my campus, gave it to her, and closed the gate; this night, she was sleeping here.

From the following morning, my life took a turn for the better, and I am indebted to Lucy for it.

"What did she do?" Meenakshi asked

I intervened. " I think I might be able to explain it better; a dog has his persona, and he has this aura around him that can change everything in your life."

"Well, I agree with you." Continued Aditya, "See, for starters, the first night she slept in my room, I felt such comfort that I wasn't alone in this world. Also, she was the first person who wasn't judging me; she only wanted to go for a walk. She didn't care about the fact that I was a junkie. Who used to spend all the money that he collected as rent on drugs and a few times went to the extent of stealing. So when she looked at me with big eyes full of love and respect, I felt something different."

The next night, seeing her trying to sleep on the floor on an old rag gunny bag that I gave her, that voice in my head said again, "She deserves better." I took out an old blanket and gave it to her, and she cuddled and slept. I didn't have any money to buy her a suitable sleeping cot, so I decided to save money and try to give her the best cot to sleep in.

The following day, when I took her for a walk, I took her to the Bagbazaar Ghat , there were some beautiful houses in the vicinity; I had seen them a million times, but that day I saw them with a different eye, Lucy belonged in these houses and not with some spoiled shit like me; I resisted the urge to buy drugs and with whatever money I had I bought some dog food and one beautiful cot for her.

Looking at her sleep peacefully that night, I heard my Dada's voice in my head, saying I am the brightest kid he knew; I started to cry loudly; I held Lucy in my arms; I missed Dada so much that day. At that moment, I decided enough is enough; I have to get back on track, and I will try to give Lucy the best life she deserves. I still have a house on my head, and I won't take that away from her.

I was just fifteen then. With the help of one of the tenants, I got admission again to a local government school; I started studying, got average grades, and managed the money well invested in the same house. Now the rent was coming a bit more. During that time, a family was living, and the man was recently appointed as a 'Registrar' and became my friend. One day, he took me to his office, and the Collector or District Magistrate was visiting his office. I saw how everyone in that office stood up as soon as he walked down the hallway; he came out of a white ambassador with two guards carrying guns and walked briskly.

Looking at him, I decided I wanted to be this guy. And my Lucy will have a big government campus to run here and there. And from that day, I started studying and preparing for UPSC.

"You don't look like a collector?" Meenakshi asked.

"No, I didn't become one; I am still studying. However, recently, I got selected as a Bank PO in the Bank of Baroda." He smiled, " I am on my way to joining the bank in Mumbai."

"Wow, what an inspiring story", Meenakshi beamed at him.

"So what about Lucy?" I asked

"Yes, she died a few months ago due to some complications. She lived for a good thirteen years. But I miss her a lot."

"So, are you planning to get a new dog?" Meenakshi asked

"No," he said

"Why?" we all asked in dismay

"She was the only one; I can't substitute her."

At that moment, I felt so emotional that a tear trickled down my eye, and I had no reply to him or his story.

Aditya put his hand around my shoulder and said, "Bro, it's time for your story".

Thirteen

WHEN THEY FINALLY MET

"Wait, after that emotional roller coaster, now I need a coffee," Shivani said.

"And I want something to eat," I added. We looked at each other to see who would get up to buy; I volunteered and went to the nearest Starbucks cafe.

Standing in the queue was a newlywed couple in front of me holding hands, too much in love with each other. Seeing them, I remembered my days and heaved a sigh about how much had changed in my life. I scrolled Instagram, and like an evil mastermind, Instagram started showing me marriage advice from beautiful middle-aged women. It was too spooky, so quickly I changed the context, and the next thing I saw was a reel of two Dalmatian dogs playing; again, how does it know the next thought in my head is about my dog?

Seeing the Dalmatians, I remembered one that came very close to Chuggi.

"Guys, here's your coffee; after all, that mellow drama. Fasten your seat belt for the next adventure in my dog's life."

Remember that beautiful Dalmatian I told you about earlier who lived close to us, the one Chuggi was eyeing for so long; his wish to be with her was about to come true.

Her name was Stella, and she was the most attractive dog in the area with her black spots, flappy ears, and big tail. Suitors from far away would come and wait outside her gate, barking and cooing, and her owner had a tough time getting rid of them. Stella lived in the back lane and usually went for walks at different times than Chuggi. Therefore, Chuggi could never see her during his walks, but only when he could go on the terrace.

The date was December 21st; that day, it was very cold; even during the day, it was freezing. The whole city was enveloped in a dense fog. The waters of the Ganga river were icy, but being 'Amavasya', many pilgrims had come to take a dip in the holy waters, so still, the city was hustling and bustling, and there was much more traffic than the usual days. You can be stuck for over two hours on such days and barely move a kilometre. Millions come to this holy city daily, but there were even more pilgrims that day.

Because of this traffic, we got home from the office late. As usual, the dog was barking like anything; he wanted to go for his business urgently. It was around 7:30 pm. Just before I could take him, it started to rain.

It was pouring heavily, but he had to go, so I quickly grabbed an umbrella and his poop scooper and left, him pulling me and me juggling two items. This wasn't my usual time, but it was the expected time for someone else's dog, who unfortunately had to take this route because of rain.

She was already there at the corner light pole. The beautiful Dalmatian.

He lifted his leg to pee, and before the first drops could touch the ground, their eyes met, and he suddenly pulled me with all his might. I couldn't control myself because the road was slippery and wet. I fell, and the leash slipped from my hand. On the other side was a frail, small girl handling the big Dalmatian. The Dalmatian also ran towards Chuggi. The poor girl tried controlling her dog but couldn't.

And they both ran towards each other. The scene was straight from a movie, with rain splashing on Chuggi's face and his ears on the side, and the Dalmatian running towards him with her tail wagging. On that winter night, two lovers would be united; it was poetic. For a moment, I was happy. And then, it hit me.

Shit, I have to stop him, or whoever will come in his way will get bitten; some tourists/pilgrims were staying close and were moving out from their hotel.

And then, behind me, another dog barked.

This was Lucky, a big black German Shepherd. He was well-trained and usually went for walks without a leash.

Chuggi used to bark at him, but he didn't care much. But today was different. A girl was involved.

Everyone has seen a dog fight, that flashing of teeth and biting. It's one thing to see it and another to try to pull the fighting dogs apart because there is only one rule in Dog fights: 'All are enemies.' This means all will fight with one another, so when two dogs fight and you try to stop them, you become a target, too. So when these three dogs started moving towards each other on that cold, drenched night, I knew the result wouldn't be good.

Chuggi reached the girl before Lucky but couldn't figure out what to do. So he started to jump on her laterally or from the front. Her owner was shouting. I had to run towards him. I picked myself up, and as soon as I started to move, Lucky zoomed past me and got hold of Chuggi's tail. And both the dogs began to fight one another; I rushed to take away my dog, but ... aaah snap, Chuggi's teeth just brushed past my foot. There was blood. Lucky's owner also came and tried to stop this fight but got bitten; after 5 minutes, we separated the dogs. Lucky was deeply hurt; blood dripped from Chuggi's tail, too. The girl stood there screaming, and the female Dalmatian ran back to her. She was fine, but the boys got hurt.

Some things are the same across the animal kingdom.

Lucky's owner came and fought with me; I fought back. Who takes a big dog, like a German Shepherd, without a leash? And my dog is only protecting himself. But still, I had to compensate him. Chuggi had very badly bitten him.

"So the poor dog was again left alone?" Shivani asked, making a sad face.

"Yes and no; someone else was watching this show from a distance that day. A beautiful brown dog was barking in the background. We named her Shiela. Apparently, by this fight, the dude had won over her."

Fourteen

FRIENDS FOREVER

When I took Chuggi for his walk the following day, a surprise awaited us. The female dog barking in the background last night came out of nowhere. And she started sniffing Chuggi's rear (A Dog's form of Hand Shake.) This made Chuggi Jump. He is not used to other dogs being friendly with him. And he sniffed her, too; there was a lot of tail wagging, and they started playing with each other.

Firstly, I was a bit worried about this friendship. Then I saw her ears clipped; apparently, it meant she was neutered, so there was no risk of any unwanted pregnancies, and like some conservative father, I was happy.

She followed us, if any stray dog came, she would run to the front and shoo them away.

After the walk, she would come to our gate and sit outside. They looked adorable together.

She was like the second dog we always wanted. Also, she was so much better than Chuggi: no uncontrolled aggression. She walked so elegantly beside us; the best part was that she wasn't afraid of anyone. We were very close to adopting her. If it weren't for our parents, we would have brought her home; she was Chuggi's first true

dog friend.

The best way to explain this walking friendship of Chuggi would be in his own words.

"Morning.. wake hooman.. useless hooman always sleeping... got to come up on bed...."

"Oh, how much time he takes in this water room.... Flussshh. Yeah, he has finished his business...."

“Take me... Take me..... You have done your business... now it's my time..... All night controlling.... Take me.....”

“This stupid leash .... Why doesn’t it take me out.... Homan hurry........Want to do my business...”

“And finally, I am out. I will fly; I will pee everywhere..... ..... This whole area is mine....... Peee here, pee there...Stupid hooman slow.......Pull harder....”

“Ohh, there you are ..Sheila... where were you ... jump on you but had to pee...”

“Looking for a place to poop.. poop .. then play..... ohh found another dog....”

“Kill you... Kill you..... but got to poop....”

“Ahh best place......finally... had to clean feat... clean feat... kick dust....”

“Ahh now Shiela.....you beautiful lick you... sniff you.....”

“Ahh, why this stupid hooman pulling me home.... Want to play.......”

“Another Dog that’s too Lucky.... You will die Lucky... die Lucky... Bite Lucky... Leave me, stupid hooman.. I will kill Lucky.”

“Shiela, where are you... why is she outside...Stupid Hoomans take her inside...”

That’s how the walks with Chuggi were or are to this day. But with Shiela also running with us, it was fun. I am sure all dog owners will agree when I say that taking your dog for a walk is rewarding.

"Here he comes back to the walking, and now it has again become rewarding; a while ago, it was a headache; you are so confused," Aditya said.

"I don't care; it's my story, my dog; please don't break the flow."

We get to move our assess and go for mandatory small walks, but still, it's a headache.

"Now it's a headache again; you are really confused," Aditya said, and Aditya and Meenakshi laughed out loud.

"It's my story, and you want to hear it. We can finish here also." I said.

"Ignore these kids, and please continue," Shivani said with a smile.

"Ok, so as I was saying.."

An always-on alarm that won't snooze; They pull, they bark. It's not us who take them out; It's them who take us out. You might think you are setting your dog's schedule, but it's them.

And then, as soon as you are out, you meet these street dogs who, like those annoying adolescent kids, just stand in the corner passing comments. My dog took every word to his heart, kept correcting those kids, and, if possible, would even run to beat them up.

In a nutshell, taking him out for his walks is tough because as soon as he sees another dog, he goes mad—mad like anything. If anyone comes in between, he is at high risk of getting bitten. On top of that, he doesn't like anyone walking behind him, and he might jump back and snarl at him or bite him.

But it's okay. These walks do have a few perks.

"Now we are back to rewards," Aditya laughed along with Shivani and Meenakshi.

My face burned with embarrassment. I gave them a look and continued.

Firstly:- My health is better:

Always wanted to get up early but need help? Stop reading these motivational books and get a dog instead. This alarm is not going off, and you have to go out. I wake up early without fail every day and started walking, jogging and doing yoga. Every morning, I curse myself; why did I get this dog? On top of that, he pulls so badly and bark, and half the time, I am scared that this stupid dog might run away and bite anyone. And I envy every other Dog owner whose dog walks so well with them.

But he takes me out of my house every day, makes me see the neighbourhood where I live, and some neighbours even start to know us. Oh, see, there goes the person with his strange dog. It also gives me time to have the most random thoughts.

I have to take him out again in the evening. The evening walks serve as a break after the office before going home, where my mind relaxes. They take out the anxiety of the day.

I always try to choose a flat near my office, and whatever the emergency in my office, I have to leave by six, max 06:30. My boss might get angry, but the little guy has to pee back home.

Secondly:- He made sure we always came back to the house.

I know he had to pee, so my outings get restricted to 6 hours max. Leaving him in the hostel/dog daycare is a traumatic experience, and in India, the lodging facilities for dogs suck! Yes, I look the other way every time I leave him. He lives in a cramped space with less sanitation and is constantly on a leash. His knees have been bruised from sitting on the floor in one position. He has gotten heavily infected with ticks and fleas and, on many occasions, has fallen sick. Plus, the trauma of leaving him is always too much. So we try to avoid it as much as possible—wherever you want to go. You will always be back. This has a positive effect in that it makes us stay more at home together, discussing things and enjoying a peaceful time together, not drenching our senses in meaningless experiences.

"The boarding for Flight No 6B534 will start in forty minutes; we appreciate your patience."

"Oh, please, complete your story, stop the preaching. You have repeated this fifty times since we met. I get it that walking your dog was hard; I am now considering getting a small breed. Move on... I want to know what happened further," Meenakshi said annoyingly.

"They might even start boarding earlier as this flight is already delayed; I want to hear the end, too," Shivani said.

"Okay, let's get back to the story."

"When I said it, it's my story. When they said let's continue. "Aditya said with a smirk.

I looked at him and whispered, "I think you know why."

Many other street dogs lived around the area, too, where I was taking him for his walk. One of them came very close to him, so much so that Chuggi even experimented with his sexuality.

Enter Rocky!

A beautiful big dog who fell in the spell of my dog, only to have his ass bitten.

During my walks, I started noticing a young white dog. He was always curious about Chuggi. But he maintained his safe distance from him. Chuggi is like I am alpha. All you other dogs are beta-gamma and delta-theta. I am the leading dog. So, any attempt by any other dog to friend him always resulted in him biting the other male dog.

But Rocky pursued. Shiela and Rocky were already good friends, and they used to play with one another. After nearly one month of Shiela becoming Chuggi's friend, Rocky also started accompanying her whenever she came towards us. However, he would maintain his distance; if any other dog came towards Chuggi, he and Shiela would run and shoo them away.

All this brought him a bit closer to Chuggi, and just like that, they started playing together: Shiela Chuggi and Rocky, Shelia and Rocky would come running towards

Chuggi. He would sit on the ground waiting for them, and as soon as they reached us, he would jump on them. I never left him without a leash. He tried running with them, but because of his leash, he couldn't, but still, he was happy. The happiness we experience in our good friends' company is just sublime.

So Rocky became his first and last male friend.

One night, Rocky came to our gate and started making noises; he was probably hungry and looking for shelter. So my wife took pity on him. She took him inside and gave him a blanket and something to eat on our porch. Seeing him, Chuggi started barking. He wanted to go out and play with him, so she left him, too, and they did zoomies together and ran all around the garden; we gave them some more food and just left them there to enjoy. By the morning, their friendship had blossomed so much that Rocky was trying to hump Chuggi.

We shooed him away. But he became a regular visitor. Both of them used to run in our backyard. It was so much fun to see them play together.

And then, on one such play occasion. Rocky peed on one of the flower pots.

Chuggi looked at him like, "How dare he do that! That's a big no. How dare he mark territory in my territory."

Chuggi ran after him, and he ran... eventually he caught him on his back. A very ugly brawl followed. Luckily, Rocky escaped by jumping our fence. And it was the end of their friendship.

So now, he used to see Shiela and Chuggi playing from the sidelines. He wanted to be part of the pack again, but it was all over for him.

Fifteen

AND SO THEY SHIFTED AGAIN

Rocky or no Rocky, for Chuggi, everything was going great; he had a big garden to run around. A great friend, Shiela. She used to sit at our gate, and Chuggi would sit on the other side of the gate during the daytime, so she kept him company when we were not there.

Things were going reasonably well for me, too. My office was now close to my home, which helped me balance my work and personal life. I loved my life here in this small, peaceful town. Additionally, my boss had changed, and he was pretty supportive. The best part was that he used to do everything by himself, which was quite impressive. Moreover, a big project was in the pipeline, and I would be the team lead. Radhika's office was good, too.

On one such fine day, we were out for a romantic date to one of the Ghats of Haridwar. Sitting beside the Holy

Ganga with our feet in the water, we felt blessed to be a part of this beautiful and holy city, seeing her waters leaving the town and going far east. Flowing in full flow and speed, she will traverse this great nation to meet up with the ocean. In the process, she will touch and purify so many cities.

I looked at my wife and said. "Our country is so beautiful. I wish we could go to the Far East, but I want to live in a bigger town this time."

"Such a random thought, but where?

"Probably Kolkatta; I have always been fascinated with its history, art & culture and socio-cultural activities, but we don't know anyone living there."

"But who cares when we have each other. Also, we can go further east, maybe to the North East, " my wife said. "My mother visited Kamakhya Temple and said Guwahati is also a lovely city."

"Yeah, it will be great", I added, and then we forgot about this small discussion and stayed till the Ganga Aarti in the evening.

It's always said to be careful with your wishes, as the universe might listen to you, and it does not distinguish between good and bad wishes.

The very next day, I heard that there would be some transfers in my office; I was confident I wouldn't get transferred because of the new project that was coming.

Then, my HR called me and asked me my preferences for the posting.

The last evening, beautiful thoughts were gone and were replaced by anxiety. I didn't want to shift and change the cities; it would be a big task. I was happy here, and my wife was also working, so she had to be transferred to the new location. Or worse, we would have to live alone in different cities.

And what about my dog? How will I take him? What will we do, as we will probably live in different cities? Who will take care of Chuggi?

This was so spooky; I should have wished for a million dollars that day, as the universe quickly responded to this wish. I didn't want to leave this beautiful city; life was so good here.

This was the second time it had happened. Previously, with respect to my boss's house, and now this. Strangely, the universe tends to listen very closely to my housing requirements.

But nothing could be done now, so I gave my preference as Kolkatta. When the universe listened to me, I thought, why not ask for what we wished for? Also, my wife's organisation had offices there, so there was a good chance we might be together.

I was nervous that day. My boss looked at me, realising I was getting worried. He tried to calm me down by telling me his stories about his transfers. And then he said, " Rishi, let's have dinner tonight at my house, maybe a last party. I heard the joining will be very soon this year; management is planning big changes. One last dinner, then who knows when we will ever meet."

This made me more nervous, so I said yes to the dinner.

I don't usually enjoy dinner with my office colleagues. I see them all day, and even after work, seeing those faces again is like the office has not ended. There, we also repeat the same things and the same issues.

Most importantly, I don't drink alcohol.

And for men, there is no party without whiskey.

So, as there was no alcohol, my boss and I discussed the usual office topics. Then we discussed my boss's postings; he had been posted in four locations, about which we had already discussed in the afternoon. We were both sitting with our wives, and all these same talks started to bore us. We even hadn't changed our office clothes.

And then, his wife suggested we go to Guwahati, a perfect city.

Hearing Guwahati, I felt like, Oh, that's the second city we thought about that day. This was unusual. Was the universe suggesting something to us?

But I had already exercised my choice. Getting Guwahati was just out of the question.

God works in strange, mysterious ways. And so does HR in companies. HR will sit in the corporate office, make us play games, dress up for functions, and have an occasional office picnic. Still, when it comes to real issues that affect employees, like salary hikes, postings, transfers, and anything that benefits employees, they are like, hmm, why should we give anything to you?

So, my posting came, and it was not Guwahati or Kolkatta. But It was Silchar, Further east of both the cities.

It was so strange. Was it the invisible hand of God or the evil mastermind HR? Why did I get Silchar? I wanted a bigger town; Silchar is predominantly a Bengali-speaking town in Assam. It was a mix of my choices and didn't seem that exciting. If God listened so carefully that day, why didn't they give me Kolkatta or Guwahati? My Haridwar was so good that I didn't want to go.

On top of that, I had to report there in a week.

With a heavy heart, I prepared to leave. Chuggi was not going with me; he was to look after my wife or my wife would now have to handle this monster. It would take another six months for her to get transferred; luckily, her office planned to set up a new branch there. Until then, I was on a forced bachelor status.

Sixteen

BOWW POWW WOWW!!

"Oh, you left your dog with your wife? That's not good. I hope she was able to handle your Cocky dog," Meenakshi said with a concerned expression.

"Where would I have taken him with me? I needed to find a new house; it was a new city, and that's too Silchar. My site office was some twenty kilometres from Silchar in a small town, Badarpur. Just try finding it on a map..."

"But seeing his photograph and hearing all about him, you shouldn't have left him with a lady. Anyhow, she had to take care of everything on her own. What sort of a husband does that? Aren't you there to help and protect her? Where has all the chivalry gone? Men these days! I remember my father was always there for my mother." Shivani joined in with Meenakshi.

" But I had a job and got transferred, remember?" I said.

"No, that was bad on your side; you should have taken him." Meenakshi Added

"Oh, ma'am, it was not his fault. She could also take him for a walk. Why do men have to do all the difficult work? You say we are equal, but for all the difficult or bad work, you are happy with Men doing it." Aditya interrupted.

"It's not like that, what I meant was..." Shivani said

"No, I know what you mean when you want us to pay on a date. On a car ride, you want us to drive. I should have more income, work hard, and provide for my family, but that doesn't apply to you." Aditya continued angrily

"Hey, Mr, what do you mean? We can do everything on our own; we don't need your lecturing about your masculinity. We were denied our positions and rights for years and faced so much societal pressure. Do you know how many women reach the top? Very few because they have to give birth and raise children, and what do men do? Sit and watch TV while we cook, make dinner, care for children, and work." Meenakshi replied angrily.

"And we work hard for our families, listen to everything the boss says, come back home, and the wife and the kids complain....." Aditya continued, and Meenakshi and Aditya came face to face; it looked like they were about to hit each other.

"Please stop! This is stupid. Both of you are just kids. You don't know what marriage looks like, so keep this online knowledge to yourself. And our flight is also about to take off, so please let me continue." I said

"Ok." Both of them said together.

"I'm sorry. I got a bit carried away. Let me buy you another coffee—hot chocolate this time," Aditya said, showing his teeth.

"Ohh, for someone believing in men and women equality, why not split it 50/50?" Meenakshi said playfully, tucking her hair behind her ears,"

"It's my way of saying I'm willing to invest in our... ongoing debate."

Meenakshi smirked and said, " Oh, is that what this is? An investment? And here I thought it was just chivalry."

"Oh, trust me, I'm all about equality. But I'm also a fan of impressing brilliant and beautiful women. You know, a little give and take."

Then they looked at each other and smiled. Meenakshi blushed a bit. How quickly this fight had turned into a cute romantic situation.

I looked at Shivani, and she murmured, "Luuvvv,"

"Ahmm, shall I continue?" I again asked, looking at them

"Ohh, please," Meenakshi said smilingly

I felt nervous about leaving my furry friend with Radhika since walking him was always challenging. He tended to pull and get worked up if he came across another pup, which I knew he would,it would be tough for Radhika to handle him. However, having our dog with us at home always gave us a sense of security. He is an excellent guard dog, always alert and able to hear any movement, which makes us feel safe, especially at night. Sometimes, it felt like he was keeping any bad vibes away, even though I don't believe in ghosts or spirits. Regardless, having him around was always a source of comfort.

Leaving this dog with her, I went to the new city.

And like a good boy Chuggi adapted to her routine; he pooped earlier, and he even woke her up a little late. He used to wait patiently for her to take him for his walks.

But he remained the same. One fine day, he did it again and got into a fight.

It's best to tell this incident in my wife's words.

"Rishi, see what your dog has done! He is a bad dog. When will he listen? You should have taken him; I was saved by the Gods today."

"Babe, what happened?"

"No, you listen first. This dog has bitten three dogs! And a miracle saved me; you remember Buddy, Teddy, Harry, the three Labradors, and their walker Negi, whom I have told you so many times to ask if he can also take your stupid dog for the walk. Well, Chuggi gave them a nice hello today."

"What?"

"What did I tell you? Listen, and always pick up the phone when I call you. So, as soon as I came from my office, he was barking so loud that he would pee then and there. He didn't even allow me to change in peace. I told him to wait, but he just kept barking. Today, it's so cold;

there is fog all over Haridwar. The paper said it's the coldest February in years! I was around the corner when Shiela came; she is so cute, we should have taken her instead of him. And then, out of nowhere, Negi Appeared with Buddy, Teddy and Harry. Because of the fog, I couldn't see them properly, and that stupid fellow had to walk close to me; whenever Chuggi sees these dogs, he barks madly, which happens every day. Still, he walked right into us. You know he pulled me so hard, I tripped and fell."

"Are you ok?"

"Okay, you should have taken him with you. You are there watching Netflix, reading books, and chilling, and here you left me. I am still okay; those poor Labradors look so cute together. He jumped on them and held one by the tail. The other tried to intervene, but he also got bitten. The third just stood there, and out of nowhere, Chuggi bit him too. All this happened before I could get up; luckily, Negi was able to separate the dogs. I gave him some rupees, and he left, but I am so mad at this dog."

"Babe, calm down."

"Calm down..." and she continued for 30 more minutes.

These three black Labrador dogs were neighbours, so their owner hired one man (Negi) whose duty was to take them out. They were opposite my dog, all so mannered, always walking in together, no pulling and pushing. Negi was so small and thin, probably in his sixties, but he could easily manage these dogs.

Their owners didn't complain much as their size saved them that night. However, the experience was too much for Radhika, so we called her parents to stay with her until her transfer orders came.

Luckily for us, within a few weeks, her request to be transferred to Silchar was accepted by her organisation.

"Hmm, I wonder what your dog felt about all this; what would be his side of the story," Meenakshi said

"Yes, the interesting part of this story," Aditya said with a smirk.

"Okay, you heard my wife's side of the story; this is probably what happened, according to Chuggi.

"Hooman tells the wrong story"... Licks his rear.

"Second Hooman Good but weak."

"Had to pee badly that day... the second hooman was late from office, pee badly."

"Stomach was aching too, so overate a lot of grass, but was still aching."

"Was missing my first hooman, then she came, forgot the first hooman, jumped on the second hooman."

"But she takes so much time to dress. Come out! I want to pee badly!"

"Okay, let's go, let's go.. find the grass. This is the best. ohh good...Want to pee more.. this is a better place; run;

I can smell the poop in this place, no, not this, Hooman, let me loose. I want to fly."

"I am the alpha; this is my place, kick dust, kick dust, kick dust. Why is she pulling? Want to kick more dust. Dogs in my territory, three dogs, will kill all of them."

"Hooman, let's go and attack. Hooman, don't pull, no time to waste... All of you must die!"

Harry- "Let's walk, I love my walk, pee here."

Buddy- "Love this walk, pee here too."

Teddy- "Who barked, that crazy dog, Harry see him, hmm this pee smell so good, oooh someone on heat... Pee smells so good."

Buddy-"Yup, pee so nice, I want her.. Why is that dog barking and running? Do something."

Harry- "Mee smell pee, I pee here, Ohh he is here, I don't like him, Boww run away, you stupid dog."

Buddy –"Ouch, he got my tail, my tail, you stupid dog. Now you are gone."

Chuggi-"This is my area; all of you bow to me or die."

Teddy-"Hooman, save us."

Chuggi- "You crazy hooman, you will die too."

Harry-"Let me show the Labrador power... Run, everyone, run."

Teddy-"The lady hooman took that crazy dog, lick the wounds."

Buddy-"Wait, but just smell this pee last time."

Chuggi: "I am the Don. No one should come in my area. Wait. I want to smell that pee, too. Hooman, stop!!!"

Seventeen

GET SET GO!

"Ooh, that must have been bad," Shivani said.

"Yeah, but she was okay."

"So what's next?" Aditya interrupted. "By the way, Meenakshi, would you like that hot chocolate ?"

"Firstly, dude, have some patience. Secondly, we would also like something to eat, and I don't mind you paying." I said

"I will have another coffee, so Capechino for me", Shivani said.

"And you Meenakshi?" He asked her again.

"Hmm, not hot chocolate, but I'll have Hazelnut cold coffee with whipped ice cream and chocolate sauce," she said, smiling.

"So you took your dog or left him?" Meenakshi asked, looking at me as Aditya left.

"I definitely took him, or else we wouldn't have this discussion here."

"Travel by air is tough for pets, so our airline doesn't take them. If anything happens to them, whose responsibility will it be?" Shivani added.

"Yes, I know that."

"Shall we wait for Aditya?" Meenakshi said

And just like that, Aditya was back after giving an order.

"What, you are starting without me? Oh, please, this story needs to end. It's like binging; I can't handle it anymore."

Most dogs are left by their owners on such transfers because transporting dogs/pets is challenging, especially over long distances. In India, there are three ways. First, we can book an AC coupe in the First AC compartment on the train. Second, we can travel by air. Interestingly, only one airline transports dogs, and it is Air India. Finally, we can travel by road.

I was considering flying to Guwahati with my pet and then taking him via road to Silchar as there was no direct flight to Silchar from Delhi at that time, but several concerns made me think twice. Firstly, my pet would have to travel in the cargo compartment, which could be uncomfortable and potentially harmful to their health due to extreme temperatures. Secondly, the pilot has the right to refuse to transport animals, and I didn't want to risk being denied boarding. Lastly, I would have to arrive at the airport three hours before the flight, which would be inconvenient. Therefore, I decided that taking a direct train to Guwahati and then going by road to Silchar was my best option.

However, I was not getting confirmed 1st Ac tickets on the direct train from Haridwar or even Delhi; The status of the tickets was Waiting 9 and 10. However, it was Waiting 1 and 2 on a different train from Delhi, so we decided to travel to Delhi by road and board the train from there.

This road journey would take 5 hours, and the subsequent journey to Guwahati via train would take another 28 hours. And then we would again go via car; I have already arranged one Innova that would take us to Silchar, which would be another 8-hour ride.

Finally, like a good husband and son, I left the arduous task of bringing Chuggi to Delhi via road to my wife and mother. From Delhi, I was joining them.

" No surprises in that". Aditya said with a smile.

Meenakshi giggled, and her smile took me back to my college days, when I would sit with friends, chatting, laughing, and not worrying about anything. Where have those days gone? At that time, I didn't like my friends pulling my leg. But now, I would give anything for just a moment like that: some close friends, a few cups of tea, some samosas and lots of laughter.

"So continuing..."

I also forgot one crucial detail: my dog hates travelling by car. He thinks he is going to the vet or being dropped off at the dog hostel, so he is scared and nervous while travelling by car.

As I said before, I had already booked two non-confirmed tickets from Delhi, with statuses Waiting List 1 and Waiting List 2 in Dibrugarh Rajdhani. I was very hopeful that this would work and that the seats would get confirmed; now, I just had to go to the Divisional Railway Manager's New Delhi Office and request him to allot us a coupe for two seats.

I also knew someone in the DRM office, and he assured me that getting a coupe would not be a problem.

I thought I had everything planned.

But life has a habit of throwing curve balls at us, and I was just about to get bowled on a googly.

And so the day arrived; I left for Delhi from Silchar, and my mother, Radhika, and Chuggi left from Haridwar to Delhi by car.

From my wife's perspective, the journey was okay, with the major issue being Chuggi drooling. But in the words of the lead hero of this story. Chuggi's journey was somewhat like this.

"Ehhh Ehhh, Huh Huh" licks his rear.

"Strangers taking my stuff. Strangers taking my hooman stuff." panting face.

" Boww, go away, protect hooman Bow, go away."

"Where have all the stuff gone? OOOOO my Hooman, come back."

"I am not liking this, not liking this. So much space."

"Ohh, no car; I don't want to go, not hostel right now."

"Ohh, this is not hostel road; this is worse, meaning doctor.", Yawns

"This is going further; want to poop right now, Hooman, stop the car."

"Ohh, I am not liking this. Let me look outside the window."

"This is good, good... ouch." And falls forward as the brake is applied.

"Finally, the car stopped; get out. Get out, Pee pee badly, Ahh poop."

"Wait, this isn't my area?? Oh, second Hooman, where are you taking me?"

"So many smells, so many places to pee... First, Hooman, where are you."

"Women, where are you going? Don't leave me in this wretched puke-inducing car.." Licks his rear.

"This taste calms me......"

"My home, where are you? I am nervous..." panting panting....

"Outside air flowing, feels good ah... want to pee-pee boww women take me out now!!"

"Ehh, so many cars, traffic can smell the tyres ,will pee on them. Women, I want to go out now."

"I love road trips; I hope to go on a road with my dog one day. And yes, now I am getting one ." Meenakshi said smilingly.

"A trip with your dog, huh? Sounds like the perfect company. But, I don't know... maybe you could use a human companion? Preferably someone who's great at arguing, paying for coffee," Aditya said

"Oh, so now you want to join me and my dog? I didn't realise 'tagging along' was part of your gentlemanly strategy," Meenakshi said, her cheeks slightly red.

Shivani looked at me and smiled jokingly. We realised that a different story was starting here.

"Yes, it sounds cute, but it was not for my wife, who was drenched in saliva that day, and my mother got irritated like anything; listen to my entire story before making any decisions."

So, somehow, they arrived in Delhi; my wife was holding him for the whole trip. If any of them went outside the vehicle during the journey, even for a second, he would panic like a small kid and bark. But still, given his standards, he was a good boy for the whole trip.

I had booked a hotel in Paharganj near platform one, as the train was supposed to leave from that platform. Everything was set.

He arrived at Paharganj in heavy traffic. Navigating the jam-packed streets, holding him tightly, I took him straight to our room. He relaxed after seeing all his family with him there.

I looked at my wife and mother sleeping peacefully after their long, arduous journey and my dog cuddled cutely in the corner of the room. I thanked God for bringing my family safely to me. At that moment, I got emotional and thanked God again for giving me such a wonderful, loving, and caring family. You can move mountains if your family is with you.

Then, the message came from IRCTC. The chart was prepared, but the tickets were not confirmed.

It's like the universe was saying, "Now it's time to move the mountain." It won't let me have one moment of peace with my family.

Now, I had to think of something else.

" You should have gone by air in the first place," Shivani said. "This was your mess."

"Yes, my mother also said the same. But in a much harsher tone. Like I said, you should plan in advance. And why are you taking this dog? Now, what will you do? I am also leaving tomorrow. You don't listen to me; this is not the game of kids; anything could have happened to us on the way. All that time, with that saliva and everything, it's so infectious."

"So what did you do?" Asked Meenakshi

"Like a good son, I didn't listen to her and complicated the things further. It was still 10:30 am, and I saw a flight

with departure at 07 pm for the same day to Guwahati by Air India; there were no direct flights to Silchar; the tickets were cheap, and seats were available but were filling fast, so I went to book, and as my mother was at me, in my haste I booked just one ticket, in the name of Radhika, as soon as I went to book my ticket, there was none available."

"Ohh, that's bad, so your wife had to take Chuggi alone ?" Meenakshi said

"Yes, but I booked a different flight for myself; the flight was to leave early at 06:00 pm and arrive at 08:45 pm, whereas Radhika's flight boarding would be around 06:25, arriving at 09:15, so I was happy; this can be managed. After all, we will go to the airport simultaneously, and the boarding is nearly identical. I will help her out by arriving early."

I quickly googled the formalities for taking a pet via air and found that I needed the following three things.

a) Rabies Vaccination Certificate (Now this I had with me)

b) Fitness certificate of the dog (This I didn't have)

c) The most important is a crate for taking the dog on the flight.

Then I googled a vet, and he was about 7 km away; he was available. I picked up my dog, got an auto, and rushed to the vet clinic.

Nothing is easy in this life. I got stuck in a traffic jam, and Google Maps directed me to the wrong location—not the clinic, but his home. To make matters worse, he wasn't there at the time. I called him, and he agreed to see Chuggi, but he was outside and would arrive in 30 minutes. Chuggi became anxious, panting and barking.

When the doctor finally examined him, he listened to my requirements and said he couldn't issue the certificate without conducting all the necessary tests on short notice. I argued that Chuggi was in good health and there were no concerns. After some negotiation and paying a bit extra, he finally agreed to provide the fitness certificate.

Now, all that was left was to find a travel crate for the dog. There are over 1,000 pet shops in Delhi, but only small crates were available wherever I went. It was now 2:30 pm, and I needed to find a crate quickly, get back to the hotel, and leave for my flight. Also, we had to leave early, as when you travel with a dog, you must reach the airport as early as possible because the dog also checks in as separate luggage and goes as cargo. Finally, the pilot needs to give consent. He can say no. The flight was from T 3, notorious for long lines and heavy passenger traffic.

I was already running late, with an effective window of one hour, and I needed help finding what I was looking for. Finally, after much googling and talking, one pet store in the Ashram area said he had it; by 03:45 pm, I got my crate and was back at the hotel.

I tried booking an Ola cab, but he cancelled when I said we have a pet dog travelling with us. The same thing happened with Uber; two autos also rejected us.

Finally, a local taxi guy agreed. By that time, my mom had already left for Bhopal. The three of us crammed in that taxi onwards for our next adventure.

By 05:00 pm, we reached the airport. We pushed Chuggi into the crate. There, he became comfortable as if he were in his new house.

"Wow, it seems like such a good adventure," Meenakshi said

" Well, the adventure didn't end here. There is still some drama left; my flight was not from T3; it was from T2."

"Oh, this means your wife had to handle all that alone?" Shivani gasped. "It can be a nightmare. "And her boarding should start by 06:25 pm, so she was with a dog at T3 with just more than one hour left for boarding. You are such a careless person; firstly, you left the dog with your mom and wife, and now, for the hard part, your wife handled all that alone."

"Yes. But.."

"Even my boyfriend is the same," Shivani added angrily

Aditya was smiling, and he and Meenakshi were giggling together.

I overlooked and continued...

After that shock, I left her at the gate and rushed for T2, only to learn that my flight had been delayed by two hours. Now I was reaching after her.

She zoomed past the initial security to check-in. Everyone was looking at her. It's not usual to see a cute dog travelling. An air hostess came close to her.

"Aww, such a cute doggie.."

"Hawww Bawww, get away... Bow Boww." snarled Chuggi. He was back in his zone.

Some kids also tried coming close to us, but they all got the response.

Chuggi was weighed with his crate, and then two Air India staff came and bravely held the crate, and he was taken away.

She constantly tried to pick up any noise from the cargo section on the whole flight. We also left him some of our old, smelly socks for relaxation.

The three musketeers sat nervously in their long flights, hoping it would end soon.

Throughout the flight, I was thinking about what Chuggi might be feeling…

"Whoaaaaa bhowwwww where am I ?"

"I will sleep..." licks his rear... sniffs, "hooman smell coming… he somewhere near."

"Me safe in this new thing... My own space..."

"So what's happening, my ears...I will chew this sock… Sock, you are dead."

"I want to pee badly. I can't control."

Thudddd... "Hmm, what's happening.. this thing is stopping..."

"Gate opening opening.. Homan, you coming'."

"Who are you? Where is my hooman... Howwww hooman."

My flight got a bit delayed and was now reaching one hour after their flight landing.

"I am wondering, did Chuggi come on the baggage belt?" Aditya asked

" We were also thinking the same; imagine a dog taking rounds on the baggage belt while everyone waits patiently for their baggage."

"Bye, the way, my luggage always comes at last," Meenakshi said

"Yes, and I always wanted to congratulate the person whose luggage came out first; that one language keeps doing rounds and rounds without anyone claiming it," Shivani added.

"Hey, if you couldn't see him, then what can we say? I always wonder where that person goes." Aditya said.

"Did you also find Chuggi on the luggage belt?" Meenakshi asked.

"No, I think he might have left him there, but as his wife, who managed everything, was in charge here, the poor dog would have been taken out in his first round," Aditya added. Meenakshi and Aditya started giggling again, and

Meenakshi even hit him on his arm. Love was really in the air or airport.

"Actually, no," I said.

Chuggi came out with an escort of four Air India Officials. They were also happy it's not like you get to handle a dog every day.

Radhika was waiting, and as soon as he saw her, he started barking

"Hoooomam... you here..... take me out!!"

"Pe peeee badly..."

"Hooman, stay close; this place is not home.. protect humans."

Finally, I also landed, and we all took a taxi straight to a hotel near the airport in the beautiful city of Guwahati, ready to start a new chapter in our lives. But before that, another eight-hour road journey awaited us.

We stayed at a hotel in Guwahati that night, freshened up, and left in the morning for the remaining journey.

The road to Silchar from Guwahati passes through the hills of Meghalaya. Poor Chuggi vomited twice, but somehow, we managed to get through and arrive at Silchar.

That night, it was very humid in Silchar. No air conditioner was installed, and my fan was also not working that well, so all three of us had to sleep on the floor.

I felt some hair on my face in the middle of the night. It was Chuggi's tail, and as soon as I opened my eyes, they fell on his 'Soron's eye,' I shifted the dog and slept again. This sight summed up our hectic journey. Somehow, we had survived this shift and were ready for the next chapter in our lives.

Eighteen

HOUSE HUNTING

Finding a new home in a new city with a dog is very tough. In India, there are other factors, too. For example, unfortunately, your surname, caste, religion and even profession matter a lot. Indian landlords are very picky.

And on top of that, we also had a lot of conditions like:-

- The flat should be on the first or ground floor, or we get an independent house. As I didn't want to take this dangerous dog via stairs or lift, he would bark at everyone and could even bite at the slightest provocation.
- The owner should not live on the same premises because a healthy dog will bark and cry every mating season. So again, you don't want to be disturbed by your owner, and

people don't understand that a dog has his ideas, problems, and desires.

- If possible it should be near the offices.
- There should be some open place to take the dog for his routine walk.
- Finally, usual like a 24-hour water supply and preferably a pretty house

My existing house was small, just one BHK suitable for a 'forced bachelor'. With me returning to my married status, we had to shift. Our household stuff was en route to Silchar, with delivery within two weeks. We needed to finalise a house in this duration.

So, as we settled in the bustling city of Silchar, a small town compared to other cities, we were determined to find the perfect rented accommodation. Given our requirements, I wish I could take Chuggi on these house-hunting adventures, too, but given his aggressive nature, I decided it was best for him alone in my forced bachelor house. I was leaving Chuggi at home with a bowl of chilled water and a cosy spot near the fan to beat the heat.

On our first day of their search, we set out with a stack of property listings. We visited a modern high-rise building called 'The Heights,'

As we explored the apartment building, we couldn't help but notice the stern expressions on the faces of some of the landlords. They asked us strange questions, like whether the dog would bark or bite. And we were like, 'no, our pet is so well-behaved; he doesn't bark and is such a good boy.'

"Ohh, that's a lie!" Aditya said

"Yes, I knew, but isn't our whole world built on promises constructed by liars,"

One after another, the owners rejected our application, citing their strict no-pets policy. But undeterred, we decided to broaden their search and explore different neighbourhoods. Our next stop was a lively 'Ambicka Patty' area with several houses and a few buildings with flats for rent. We entered the cramped hallways of an old 'Mini Manor' building, hoping it would live up to its charming name.

As we toured the building, I couldn't help but imagine Chuggi zooming through the narrow corridors, tail wagging with excitement.

However, when we inquired about bringing Chuggi, the owner, Mr. Sen, frowned and shook his head disapprovingly. He expressed concerns about the potential damage dogs could cause in such a compact living space. We even pleaded with Mr. Sen, promising to take extra care and responsibility (as the place was perfect) for Chuggi's behaviour, but our efforts seemed futile.

Disappointed yet determined, we continued our search. We hopped from one place to another, facing rejection after rejection due to Chuggi's presence; at this moment, you feel, 'Why did we get this dog in the first place.'. We could feel the sweat trickling down our foreheads in the scorching heat of Assam, and it was very humid that day, but we had to keep our spirits high.

Finally, as the sun set, we stumbled upon a charming, well-ventilated apartment building called 'Gopal Residency.' The name somehow felt assuring as fate led us to our ideal home. The owner, Mr. Baid, welcomed us warmly and listened attentively as we explained our desire to bring Chuggi with us.

Mr Baid was a well-known businessman in Silchar; He was practical. He didn't care about the dog; the only thing that mattered to him was that the rent should go to him on the 1st of every month. He already had prepared a lease agreement that was ready for signing.

Relieved and overjoyed, we signed the lease, grateful to have found a practical landlord who embraced our furry family member. We brought Chuggi into our new home; he explored every corner curiously, tail wagging in approval.

Nineteen

LOVE IN THE AIR

"It's absolutely adorable how all three of you have made yourselves at home in a new city!" Meenakshi exclaimed, her eyes sparkling with excitement.

I looked at her and thought, In hindsight, everything looks so good and breezy, like a song, but at that moment, things were so hard, coming to a new city and office. It was hard for my pet too. The voice of the air hostess broke my thoughts; what was her name? Oh, my teenage self would be so ashamed today. I forgot the name of a beautiful lady; I tried looking for her pin; why do these people put their pins in a place we are not supposed to see?

"Do you know who I am? I am Shivani Kapoor, and my father is..." she yelled. Thank God she screamed her name.

"Well, Shivani, what happened?" I asked

"It's my landlord; not every landlord is as good as yours. Mine's a real jerk. As I said, I started listening to your story because my boyfriend 'Ravi' suggested getting a pet. But we are not living together, so I didn't give much thought to his idea, but he persisted and said we could take care of him together. Sometimes he can stay at my house, sometimes at his house. This idea was so impractical. We had this talk around two months ago. Lately, I have been thinking about this crazy plan again. My current house is big, and my boyfriend stays close to me maybe It can be done."

"I asked about bringing a pet with my landlord, but he said no. And he again called me saying he won't allow any such thing. He also has a problem with my boyfriend coming. After hearing your story, I have decided I want a pet now at any cost. I think it will also bring Ravi and me closer." There was sadness in her eyes. Seeing a sad, beautiful girl, I jumped to console her—some things I suppose never change.

"So, how did you meet this Ravi? Meenakshi asked.

"Ohh, leave it. Let him finish his story first." She said.

"Arey, his story is very long; I have no hope it will be completed before this flight takes off. And I think Meenakshi has already decided to get a dog. You are, too, getting a dog; there is no point in his storytelling. We are all strangers here; we will not judge you, so please feel free to share your love story." Aditya said.

I again felt violated by Aditya's comment, but her sadness and beauty were so captivating that I couldn't help myself saying this.

"Yes, probably this story can take a break."

I grew up in Gwalior, a small town that holds tightly to its traditions. As a young girl, I often found myself staring up at the sky, mesmerised by aeroplanes that soared above. While most people around me were content with their routines and plans of settling down, I had a different dream—to become an air hostess and see the world. It felt impossible, but my heart wouldn't let the idea go. When I was 12 years old, I sat on my first flight and saw the crew at work. I decided then that I would be an air hostess at any cost.

My family didn't understand my ambitions. 'Girls like you don't belong in such flashy professions,' my father would say over and over again. He had other plans for me; no matter how much I tried to explain, they couldn't see beyond society's narrow expectations. It broke my heart, but I knew that if I stayed, my dreams would wither away.

One night, after yet another heated argument, I made the hardest decision of my life—I decided to leave. With just a small backpack and a few hundred rupees I had saved, I boarded a train to Mumbai, the city of dreams. I was terrified but also filled with a strange sense of freedom. For the first time, I felt in control of my destiny.

Mumbai was overwhelming. The noise, the people, the never-ending hustle—nothing like Gwalior. But I couldn't afford to be scared. I quickly found work at a small café in Kurla, where you could see aeroplanes taking off and landing very close by, pulling long shifts to make ends meet. It wasn't glamorous, but it allowed me to survive and save up for the real reason I came here—to enrol in an air hostess training program.

The nights were the hardest. After exhausting work hours, I would study by dim light in the small room I rented. I'd fall asleep with my books, dreaming of what it would feel like to be on an aeroplane, serving passengers, smiling, and travelling to places I'd only seen in magazines.

There were moments when I doubted myself. Days when the city felt too big and my dreams too far out of reach. But every time I saw a plane take off from the nearby airport, I knew I was exactly where I needed to be. I reminded myself why I had left home, which gave me the strength to keep going.

Months passed, and after countless lessons, tests, and late nights of studying, I finally completed my training. I couldn't believe it when I received my certificate. It felt surreal—like the entire world had opened up before me. Then came the day I had dreamt of for so long: my first job offer as an air hostess. I remember clutching the letter, tears streaming down my face, knowing everything I had worked for was finally becoming real.

When I stepped onto that plane in my crisp uniform for the first time, I felt like I was flying even before takeoff. The passengers smiled at me, and I greeted them confidently, knowing I had earned every bit of this moment. I wasn't just a girl from Gwalior anymore; I was someone who had fought for her dreams and won.

A few years later, I returned to Gwalior—not as the runaway daughter my parents feared they had lost, but as a successful, confident woman. When I stood in front of my family in my airline uniform, I could see the surprise and pride in their eyes. They hadn't understood before, but now they did. I had followed my heart, and it had led me to places I couldn't have imagined.

With all of this, I never had any time for love or relationships. Also, the airline industry is very competitive and demanding, so I was busy with my world. Love and companionship had taken a back seat.

Then, one fine day on a flight from Delhi to Mumbai, I was part of the crew on the plane. Due to some staff shortage, I was also doing duty for boarding at the airport exit gate.

One young gentleman was sitting in the corner near the gate with headphones on; I looked at him once and thought he looked cute.

The boarding was about to be completed, and we noticed that one Mr Ravi hadn't boarded yet.

"This is the last and final boarding call for Mr Ravi."

There has been no response for five minutes. This is the part of my job that I hate the most. It feels so stupid, like you have to run after small kids. A few are so eager to board that they will stand for three hours, and we must repeatedly tell them to sit. And then some get lost in the crowd.

I glanced again at that man patiently reading his book, and he looked up. Our eyes met, and my heart skipped a beat.

And then he looked here and there, and I knew there was Mr Ravi. I shouted, "Last and final call for boarding to Mumbai."

And he came running; he smiled innocently, and I gave him a sarcastic smile, and the boarding was complete. And then, just before the take-off, the flight developed some glitch, and there was a delay. I am terrified of these waits because people get nervous sitting in a stationary plane; everyone wants to get down. A few wanted to go to the washroom, but the captain had switched on the seat belt signs, so we had to stop them. And the flight was not taking off.

That flight like this one was also delayed at the start; a few passengers had a connecting flight, and they started getting angry and shouting; the situation was getting out of hand, and someone had taken out his phone to record the whole situation. I felt my temper rising, and at that moment, I wanted to say to those passengers, 'Let me accept your request and let this plane fly (as though I had that in my hand). And If something happens, I will jump from the parachute, and you will die.' But I maintained my air hostess smile. The matter was getting serious, and we were about to inform the airport authorities.

And then, like a hero, Ravi intervened with all his chill vibe. He stood up and tried to soothe things; he was 6 feet 2 inches. His size was such that people accepted his opinion and stopped shouting; something about him seemed magical. Our eyes met again, and he smiled as he smiled at me at the airport; I smiled back nervously. There was an instant spark.

When the flight landed, he remained seated patiently and was one of the last passengers to get down; I thanked him and said, "Goodbye, have a good day." I wished I could see him again, but I knew that happens only in the movies.

Then suddenly, I had an idea, so I ran up to him and asked, "Can you give feedback? I am Shivani; please mention my name." I didn't care about the feedback, but I thought we might have some conversation by doing this. But he smiled and went away.

Well, I again saw him at the baggage belt, patiently waiting for his baggage; I remained there looking at him from a distance like a teenager.

He took his bag and came straight towards me. Our eyes met again, and I smiled and asked him, "Have you given that feedback?"

"Yes, I will give, but I am a bit hungry. you didn't even give any free food on the flight, given it was delayed." He said

"Oh, my bad. If you don't mind, please come with me to that restaurant. It has the best sandwiches you can find at any airport."

"You mean cold and pricy?"

"No, they will be hot and about price, don't worry, it's on me; no, I meant the airline," I said with a nervous smile, and that's how our story started.

"Okay, so that's the way to impress air hostess," Aditya added

"Dude, Ravi was 6 feet 2; Shivani, please continue," I said.

"We have been in a relationship for some time, and it's good, but lately, we have some differences. So maybe getting a dog might take our relationship to the next level, so..."

"Then get engaged and Marry," I said.

"No, I am not ready for that yet, neither is he. But we can raise a pet together and see how it goes."

"Oh, that's why you want a dog: to see how it feels like a family. What will happen to the poor creature if you break up? I suggest going for a fish instead."

"That's what Ravi is suggesting now. It was his initial idea, but now I am thinking about it, and after hearing your story, my determination to get one has strengthened."

"I don't understand why you still don't get it. Getting a dog is easy, but taking care of him is another story. Make up your mind after I finish my story; the real challenge is yet to come."

"Then complete your story." Meenakshi said, "The boarding can start anytime now."

Twenty

"SABA KICHU BHĀLA CHILA"

Before Kabir, my son came into our lives, 'everything was good' for Chuggi. As per GENZ lingo, we were in the 'DINKWAVSD' financial category. That is Dual Income, No Kids with a Very Spoiled Dog. He was the pampered kid of the house, and all the attention was on him. Every evening, we used to play together, with him doing zoomies and running here and there, sometimes with my sock or a used plastic bottle. Also, he was free to move about in the house; only the kitchen was out of his reach.

For Chuggi, his life was the same, wake up early, bark at me and go pooping, bark again and sleep. But this location brought some new challenges for him. Firstly, living in an apartment meant no garden to run around and no emergency peeing location—just a tiny balcony overlooking the road. There were new dogs and new smells. However, the most significant issue he faced was during his evening walks. When I saw this apartment, I realised there would be issues as the flat was located on the main street and was very crowded. There was an empty by-lane, and the road had just been made, so the people were susceptible to the looks of that road. And pet owners in India, well, we suck. We don't carry the poop-scooper, and our dogs shit where they like and pee wherever they want, and even when I was having the scooper, they still objected to Chuggi going there.

So, the only road left was the main road with all the shops and offices, and it was one of the main connecting roads in the city. In the evenings, on most days, there would be a traffic jam on that road. Unfortunately, the street lighting was also not that good on that road. And my dog liked to poop just where it was darkest.

But still, that could be managed. My main issue was that there were many street dogs.

The best way to explain this situation is by walking with Chuggi.

It's 06:30 pm, and I am back from the office. Chuggi is all set to go out for his walk, and he is jumping and overtly excited; I tie his leash, and off we go.

Upon leaving the compound, we are met with a long line of jammed cars, leaving us with no choice but to use the footpath. The footpath is bustling with people constantly coming and going. Depending on the traffic movement, I must hold my dog tightly and shift him from left to right. Suddenly, a person appears straight before us, causing me to move my dog to the other side. However, my attention was soon diverted to a beautiful girl coming from her college who needed saving from this dangerous situation. I wait around the corner of the footpath with Chuggi facing the boundary wall. As soon as the girl and the random person passed, we resumed our journey, only to be greeted by a group of chatty aunties occupying the whole path. I must push my dog to the side again and hold onto him till the aunties pass.

"You know you look like an uncle." Meenakshi interrupted

"And his hair is also grey with that tummy," Aditya added

"Agreed," said Shivani with a smile.

I overlooked that conversation and continued.

And then, behind that group of aunties, hidden from my view, a street dog walks straight towards us.

Chuggi sees him, and he starts to growl, and before I can realise what's the issue, he starts barking, with his mouth moving at the speed of sound, and anything that comes in the way of these teeth will be bitten /broken or torn. Now I have to save the aunties. Luckily, they see him and get down the footpath, but there is a lot of commotion on the road. And that stupid dog is still coming towards us; I frantically try to find a piece of stone to scare the other dog; luckily, he backs off, and I continue with my dog pulling and pulling in search of a remote light pole with some dirt or grass on the ground so that he may relieve himself, but he doesn't. So now I have to go to the other side of the road on the next footpath as the following good location for his pooping is there. But the same dog is there, too, and again, the brawl starts.

This was my everyday evening struggle, but God forbid any pet dog came my way; it became a nightmare because I couldn't scare him with a stone, as his owner would object. Also, he is not disturbed by Chuggi's aggressive behaviour, as most pet dogs don't face such a situation.

In such situations, my only option is to change my route or take him back.

However, there were no significant issues in the morning as there was no traffic, so I could easily control him.

One particular dog made Chuggi very hyper. He was a beautiful golden retriever named Simba, who always walked alongside his owner.

On seeing Simba, he used to get so angry that he would stand on his two feet and bark his heart out.

Initially, Simba didn't take any notice, but then he was like Whooo Whooo Shoo Shoo.

These Golden retrievers look so cute even when they are angry.

"I was thinking." Aditya intervened, "Do you even work or just stay home with your dog? You are so obsessed with his walks."

"Shh, let him continue," Meenakshi said. I looked at him with the same look as the Bald Pakistani cricket supporter

who became famous on the internet, with his hands on his waist after his team lost against India.

Their everyday engagement was so intense that they were engaged in some bow-wow rap battle whenever they faced each other.

"Bhoww Woww, I am the don of this area."

"I will Kill you, Simba, if you don't leave this area."

"Who woo, look at my hair, you stupid dog."

"I don't talk to rascals; go bark at another dog."

"Bhoww Woww, I will eat these long brown hairs."

"Who are you? Even your hooman is scared."

"You are black, and I am brown."

"I look cute even when I frown."

And this continued for a while; this bow-wow rap battle attracted some young female dog crowd.

"Surely Simba looks handsome, but this Chuggi can protect us, but Simba will give cuter babies."

A local dog also joined the crowd.

"Babes, their thing will never reach your things, but I'm also scared of this Chuggi; he is my role model."

For me, this show was a monument of embarrassment. More than embarrassment, I feared what would happen if he broke his leash and attacked the poor dog and owner. So I was always on the lookout for Simba and used to change my route as soon as he was in my view; still on the corners and around the turns, I would sometimes encounter him, and they would again engage in the same rap battle.

"That seems like an adventure," Meenakshi said.

"Adventure? Were you not listening? No, it was bad; I always walked with him in fear. And sometimes my wife and Mother also had to take him."

"Okay, but still, this could have been managed," Shivani added.

"Yes, I was trying my best. After a few initial months, I got settled in the routine; Chuggi also settled, but it was all from over; the real trouble was about to start."

Twenty-One

BARKS AND ROSES.

But before that, It's time for the next lady in the little Dude's life. Enter Munni.

A beautiful and street-smart dog, she was brown and looked super cute. She knew her area on the street and her place to eat was fixed; she stayed away from traffic, hung out with the most robust dog in the vicinity, and was always happy. People generally loved her, and she didn't bark uselessly.

The moment her eyes fell on Chuggi, she followed him everywhere. She would always trail behind him, and as soon as Chuggi would leave the building, she would come running towards us, just like Shiela. At first, I thought maybe she, too, had fallen under Chuggi's spell, but no, she wasn't as naive. She was a very intelligent dog.

Street dogs have a complex social hierarchy, and living on that street was difficult. It was filled with people traffic, a bustling marketplace with space constraints. Moreover, eight to ten dogs fought for food and resources, making the competition fierce. The toughest dog among them (even Chuggi left him alone) was a white dog, but he was getting a bit old.

Lastly, there was a couple, a doggie couple. Let's call them 'la Familia'; they were quickly becoming the new power centre in that area.

There was this one local chicken shop, and it was the battleground for the dogs. The strongest got all the meat; the bones were left for the smaller and weaker ones.

The older white dog was sidelined in a few months, and this 'la Familia' was now controlling this area. They were perfect; I had never seen such a dog family. We named them the smiths. When other strays tried their luck, Mr Smith's alone was usually enough to send them scurrying. But if they were stubborn, Mrs Smith would step in, her graceful but menacing posture saying, You don't want this fight, friend.

The shop staff loved them, often referring to Mr and Mrs Smith as their unofficial security team. No cats dared wander near the kitchen bins, and delivery drivers made quick, respectful stops, always knowing to throw a bit of food as a peace offering.

Mr Smith was a scrappy, street-smart mutt with a scar over his left eye; Mrs Smith was a beautiful white and brown bitch but with an attitude of a queen. They also had a small brown puppy with big ears whose leg got hurt in an accident, so he was limping but still healthy.

Now, Munni was the older, white dog's favourite. She was there too until he was around the chicken shop, but as soon as he was out of the picture, Mr and Mrs Smith took over the area. Mrs Smith started shooing her away, but Munni didn't pick up a fight with her; she stayed near the shop, picking up scraps.

In this situation, like a movie star with one leg in the air, pee drops touched the pole near the Chicken Shop and, with his hyper dirt kicking, entered my rowdy dog!

"Ooh, this is getting interesting," said Meenakshi

I should tell this part of the story from Chuggi's perspective.

"Thank you, I will again say it, dude, your storytelling sucks," Aditya said with a laugh.

"Bhmm...I shifted to a new house, loved it, had more space to run, and loved the balcony. Bowww, Bowww."

"Hooman sleeps late here. And it's hot; I wake early, and Hooman still sleeps."

"More places to pee, but Hooman pulls me away; I want to sniff and lick more. So many babes here, all hot and ready for me."

"Will rule this place just this stupid leash stopping me, hooman leave me."

"Munni I love her, Boww. She is good, stupid hooman not leaving me; if he leaves me, I will give him so many Chuggi Puppies."

"Munni follows me. I sniff her.. hmmm, HOOMAN, please leave me once."

"But there is this Mrs Smith. Hmm, she is Bhowww wow, But hate Mr Smith will kill him bite him, and then give human Chuggi puppies from Mrs Smith too."

"Hooman, what will he do without me, bowww my biggest enemy...Grrrrrr... What was his name.. Tiger, will Bowww Kill him."

"Love the Smith kid, want Mrs Smith, kill Mr Smith."

Tiger was the old white dog, as I mentioned before. He was also around, although he had lost his territory. He was in love with Munni and followed her everywhere; he was like she was my girl. But she didn't care and was eyeing Mr Smith.

Chuggi changed the power struggle in the area.

So, Smiths controlled the area around the chicken shop. Munni was living on scraps, and Tiger was usually around the other chicken shop, but it was small; the route of my dog's walk was from one chicken shop to the other. So, all four dogs came into the purview of Chuggi.

As soon as this dog did his first pee and kicked the dust storm sending his pheromones and hormones in the air for all the bitches out there, the first babe to notice this half husky and half German shepherd aggressive dude was Munni and came wagging her tail behind, and head tilted to her side.

Chuggi gives her one look and continues forward.

She followed us just like Shiela, but she was different. She was not following us unthinkingly; she was always looking out for other threats and bigger dogs. Then we reached the chicken shop, which was located on the main road.

Silchar is a large, bustling town but still smaller compared to other Indian cities, and its streets and roads, just like any Indian city, tend to get congested with traffic. The chicken shop was at the junction of a smaller connecting lane meeting the big busy road 'Satsang Road'; the road was not that big but was still very busy with cows, trucks, busses, and vehicles everyone on that road. Our house was on a parallel street. In the mornings, down this road, it was good. But in the evenings, it was a nightmare. I kept him on a tighter leash and then started using two leashes to be sure if one failed.

Mr and Mrs Smith used to sit on the first floor of the shopping centre balcony behind the chicken shop. (I think they probably thought of themselves as the rulers of that area.) So, as soon as Chuggi approached them, both started shouting from above. Chuggi looked at them, and all his hair stood up, and he barked and barked, his teeth flashing and mouth moving at the speed of sound.

Then Mr Smith and Mrs Smith came down. I had to pick up some stones to shoo them away, as it created a lot of commotion; they both went up again and resumed their barking.

All this made Munni very happy; she had found a new hero. This evening, she would be dining at the prized location.

A new boss was in the town.

And so, every time after that, if Chuggi went in front of the chicken shop, she would come there. Chuggi would bark mainly at Mr Smith, and he used to bark from the first floor and not come down to face him directly. This was changing the power equation in this chaotic dog world.

Mrs Smith was smart, and she understood what was happening. After a few days, she stopped barking at Chuggi and instead turned all her attention to Munni. As soon as Munni became visible, she would run after her and shoo her away.

But Munni was more intelligent; she increased her closeness to Chuggi. She started to walk closer to us. As soon as Chuggi exited the building, she would run towards him and walk closely to us. Because of Chuggi, Mrs Smith couldn't shoo Munni away, and that's how she got a front-row seat at the chicken shop.Finally, the mating season arrived.

The girl was in love and just wanted her hero, but he lived in a building, and she was on the streets; suitable suitors started coming from far land (nearly eight dogs appeared), and one was Tiger.

He was such a beautiful dog. Although he looked old, he would have made a lovely pet dog.

And he knew how to handle an aggressive pet dog like Chuggi.

Firstly, he wasn't scared of him. He knew that this guy was on the leash, and there was no way he could harm him. So to piss Chuggi off, whenever we used to cross him, he used to follow us closely; he never barked at Chuggi but would pee at all the places Chuggi did his business. Chuggi, on seeing this, would bark very loudly, but he didn't care. He just used to show one or two teeth and kept walking close to him, teasing him. He would still trail us even if I tried to scare him.

Second, when Munni used to run towards Chuggi, he ran behind Munni, and Chuggi would pull me hard and bark at Tiger, so to have his walk in peace, I had to shoo Munni away. This was a win for him. Now his babe can't come near Chuggi.

At times, I feel that I was being so cruel to Chuggi that I didn't allow these two lovers to meet, with Munni sitting in front of my colony gate.

Then, one day, it happened.

"So Chuggi got loose, and ahmm ahmm," Meenakshi said with a naughty smile.

"No .."

How long would a beautiful girl wait? Her best friend, Tiger, was there to support her. So, the tiger fulfilled all her needs, and poor Chuggi was left on the balcony, where he saw everything with his eyes. He gave those painful barks, but it was too late.

"Ehh, the best friend", Aditya murmured angrily. "Meenakshi, your best friend?."

That was so cringy; I gave him a disapproving look and continued.

He didn't have food for a few days. After that, she got pregnant and gave birth to beautiful brown puppies who followed us with their mother, but whenever they tried to go too far, she made them return to their home in the basement of a building. The puppies loved Chuggi, and he was happy playing Uncle. Tiger went away mysteriously to hunt for some other damsel. The friendship between Chuggi and Munni did remain.

Twenty-Two

THE FIRST BLOOD

"Your dog handled the rejection so gracefully," Shivani said.

"Ohh yes."

"I am still unable to get my head around one thing: it's clear you love your dog, you have monitored his every feeling, and you went all the way to bring him to another city. So why are you still opposed to me having a dog?" Meenakshi said.

"You are right. Now starts the uncomfortable part; my dog would do something horrific and unforgivable around this time."

As we settled into our new life in Silchar, so did Chuggi. We even found one fantastic cook, Vijaya, who was regular. We loved her. She was punctual, didn't take any leaves and made the perfect North Indian food here in the Northeast.

There was but one problem that we knew about, but we still took it lightly. Our dog is a perfect guard dog; he had one rule: no one except my family in the house, so he would constantly bark at all our cooks and housemaids even when they had been coming to our home for more than a year. He didn't like anyone entering our house except the house members. However, this is an excellent quality with a guard dog. The problem is he not only warns but attacks at the first chance.

We usually sat in our drawing room every night after returning from our offices, had tea together, and sometimes played with Chuggi. When Vijaya used to come, we kept him on a leash or close to us.

That evening was my birthday, and my wife had just ordered a smartwatch for me. She showed it to me, and we got distracted and moved into our bedroom. Chuggi was left in the drawing room without his leash.

And Vijaya came outside the kitchen to ask for something, and he just attacked her. He bit her in her stomach; blood was everywhere, and she was crying like anything.

We had to rush her to the hospital immediately; her family also came, and although we paid for all the treatment, it wasn't close to the trauma the lady had to endure. For days, she couldn't sleep properly. We got distracted, and this dog didn't even warn us. We felt so guilty and didn't know what to do.

We also got scared of Chuggi. But we knew it was our fault. Chuggi constantly barked at her; we got careless, but our carelessness caused her so much agony. Yes, we did everything for her treatment. I tried to give her the best medicine, but that horror in her eyes will always haunt me.

After a few days, we forgot our guilt, and life moved on. COVID came and went, but Chuggi was still there; on those empty streets, I walked with Chuggi alone. There were also protests. A curfew was imposed, tyres were burnt, and rallies were taken. We both still walked those empty streets.

And then we were blessed with a beautiful baby boy. We named him Kabir.

Twenty-Three

I WISH...

"It must be horrible for the lady," Meenakshi said

"Yes, that scene is still in front of my eyes. We love our dog like anything. So even after this incident and Kabir, Chuggi was still with us."

And then he did it again.

"This time, our maid, Mehrunissa, got bitten—and again, without any fault of hers."

There was the same horror in her eyes, and we took her to the best doctor and paid for all her injections, as we did with Vijaya. But the guilt was there; after all, it was our fault. Her wounds were far worse. My neighbour came and looked concerned; he had a small kid and was worried for his safety.

"Right now, your child is small, but when he grows old and will run here and there, what will you do? Are you confident with this dog? Plus, when he has his friends who will come every day to your house, how will you control all that?"

I had no answer to that question; I couldn't look into Mehrunisa's eyes after this incident. It was all my fault; even thinking about it filled me with guilt and remorse. In my panic, I decided to leave this area. And settle some other place.

Radhika said, "You are stupid. No, this dog is going. We are not shifting. It's a matter of life for my kid. It ends here. If you don't leave him, I will leave. I am terrified."

"But... but... he has been with us... "

"Does our kid matter or this wild dog? He is not going to change. And now you are still defending him."

"We have received this gift after such a long time. It's about him. I won't let that dog come near my grandson." My mom retorted.

Then my sister came to visit me. Her visit was like a light breeze. Her presence reduced the stress a bit, and I took her to the banks of Barak River, a big tributary of the Mighty Brahmaputra. A lone fisherman was fishing with a light breeze hitting our faces. It relaxed me.

"Bhaiya, what will you do now?"

"I am thinking", I replied.

"Some things just can't be avoided; you have to take a decision and go with it. Not taking any decision will harm you. It's not what will happen but what might happen, and thinking all about it is harmful. Just get the things done. Either give him away or own him and ensure he doesn't bite Kabir. Make sure there is a proper boundary between them. But remember, Kabir will always come first. Bhabhi is right here, and changing the house is not the solution."

I don't know how it happened, but the universe was listening to my changing house talk gain. The next day, after my sister and I were sitting at the ghats of Barak River, my transfer orders came. This time, even the HR didn't ask; it was so sudden. The new location was on the opposite side of India, Jodhpur. It was as if the universe thought, "Let's have some fun. Let him now feel the heat of Rajasthan after the humidity of Assam."

On top of that, my sister accidentally stepped on Chuggi's tail while he was sleeping; he snapped and bit her legs. It was more of a warning, but enough for some blood to come.

It was enough now; from that day onwards, Chuggi was shut in the balcony or his crate; it seemed everyone hated that dog.

But deep in our hearts, he was still the same for us. That same aggressive butt licking cute fur ball. Even though my wife wanted him to go, she loved him too much, and the thought of leaving him was disturbing for both of us.

But we knew he had to go now. We had to leave this dog here. This dog won't understand a thing and will always wait for me.

Radhika also applied for the transfer. And she was moving with me too.

We came here as three, and now we were leaving as three.

My options were limited; I could leave him in a jungle a day before my flight.

This option was easy. I thought he could easily survive in the wild, but we know he will come back here, and when the locals see him, they might harm him, or worse, he might get hurt. I didn't dare to do it. The thought of my dog running after me, searching for me, gave me chills.

The second was we could give him up for adoption; we tried finding one but couldn't find any adoption centres in Silchar. Plus, as he was eight years old. We tried Olx and quicker Facebook ads, but no one was willing to take him.

My only option now was to leave him with a breeder and pay him a monthly boarding fee. One of Radhika's friends, who lives in Bangalore, also faced the same situation. She gave her dog to a local breeder for a monthly fee when she got pregnant. This option seemed our best possible choice in this situation.

But we were living in Silchar, and not Banglore. Such things were unheard of here. Anyway, this seemed the best option. So, with a heavy heart, I called the hostel guy where we usually left him. He refused flatly and got angry, asking why I was destroying my dog's life. He is such a good boy.

Then there was one more guy. With him, I left Chuggi just once. Chuggi returned bruised, so I didn't go again with him. But he was more professional and had a lot of space for the dogs.

My whole body was telling me not to do this, but I had no other option. We had to leave in a few days.

The deal was made. I agreed to pay him some upfront money and monthly boarding fees of Rupees Five thousand.

On his last night with us, we couldn't sleep; we cried a lot. He has been an integral part of our lives. He is home to us. He is our first kid.

We packed all of his belongings in the morning. I included a box of his favourite milk bones in his bag. My tears wouldn't stop. I glanced at my wife; she was also in tears.

I knew he was nervous. He always is, but this time, he was a bit calmer; probably, he sensed something.

But we were not. I heard him barking as I handed him over and gave money to the owner of the dog hostel. My heart was beating like anything. I knew this was wrong, but it had to be done. The poor dog would wait for me for his entire life. I am not bad, but what other choices did I have?

I didn't say anything that day to anyone and got busy packing. How can I leave him like this? He is my kid. Even in my darkest times, he was the only constant part of my life. What sort of a person I am, I couldn't do one thing correctly. I had no right to give an innocent animal so much pain.

But... my kid matters more.

With a heavy heart, we packed and left the bustling city of Silchar.

I wish he weren't this aggressive; I could have trained him properly, and he could be the best buddy to my kid. Every boy should have a dog, and my boy also deserves one. And my dog also deserves better pet parents. I wish we could all be together always.

Twenty-Four

THE LAW OF KARMA

There was complete silence around; no one was speaking.

"You left the dog alone and helpless. That's incredibly cruel and irresponsible." Meenakshi said

"No, he did right." Aditya said, "his kid's life mattered more, and as per his story, this dog is very aggressive."

"But he didn't bite any family members and only attacked the outsiders. Don't you want these qualities in a dog? He could have waited and seen how his kid and dog behaved around each other and then taken this step," Shivani said.

"Well, I am leaving and feeling disgusted after hearing all this; the poor little dog must be waiting somewhere for him to return. Goodbye Mr Rishi."

I looked at her and said, "Wait, before you judge me so severely, the story is still not over."

Meenakshi stopped. She looked at the boarding line and said, "I get your point about why I should not have a dog, and after this, what is left to hear? And anyways, the boarding is about to start."

"Yes, you are right. That was the reason why I said not to get a dog initially. I never thought I would be sharing this story with anyone. If you want to know whether to have a dog or not, this is all I have to share, but if you want to know the meaning of love with your pet, you need to know how this story ends."

"Please, Meenakshi, sit; there is still time. Let's hear what more is left of his story," said Shivani.

Meenakshi looked at me disapprovingly and sat down grudgingly. "Please say what else you got to say; we have to board the plane."

"By the way, I also have to board the same plane."

On the flight, I kept telling myself I did the right thing. It's important for my kid; now, he can happily crawl around. No hairs, no one barking in the morning.

Suddenly, I saw a hair on my shirt, black and brown hair with a tinge of white on the tip. With its wavy texture. These hairs have been a part of our lives. Now I have left them—no more messy hair on the clothes or the bed. There will be no need to comb him; things will be clean. There will be no dirty paws around. There would be no drop of saliva around and no occasional vomiting. My child will grow in a clean and healthy environment. And no more of that doggy smell.

No more of those random barks at night for asking for treats, no more of that curious face.

No more jumping on me when I come back. We can go wherever we want. No more seeing those big beautiful eyes asking why you are leaving me in this house alone and when you will return.

But they will be searching for me. Those big ears will always be strained for the sound of my car, and that nose will always be searching for that home smell.

Oh, he has grown old. I thought to myself.

But he is still eight. There are years ahead. He is in good shape.

Shut it up!!!!

I closed my eyes and cried softly.

My wife wasn't better either. We both had hardly spoken to one another since we boarded the plane.

I looked into her eyes... And she started to cry.

"I miss him; we are such bad people, Rishi."

"I know but....."

This was my turn to cry. I cried in big sobs, and people around me looked at us. We men don't cry, but when we do, we don't know what to do about it. It's like some tap has been left open.

"How can I be so selfish? He never asked us to keep him. But we decided to have him, and now we are abandoning him. What does this make me? I am not this."

"But now we can't do anything; we must take this guilt to our graves."

We departed from Silchar with heavy hearts, joining millions of pet owners who leave their pets behind.

We started looking for our new house within a few days of reaching Jodhpur. Getting a perfect home in a new city is always challenging, but we didn't have a dog this time, so people were more accepting of us. There was no stress, no need to take him out, so we took the flat in the middle of the city, just in front of my wife's office.

No one was waking me up early in the morning, so I started getting up by eight. We hired a lady to care for our kid, so our parents also got free. Also, I wasn't obligated to come home early to take Chuggi out. I got promoted, and the workload and responsibility increased.

Time is the biggest healer; after one month, we left the memories of Chuggi behind, or so I thought. In between, whenever Google Photos showed me a memory of Chuggi, I tended to avoid it.

Our parents were also happy as they could now come and go at their discretion. Because of my dog's nature, we could not keep a Nanny, but now that wasn't the issue.

I still missed him, though. Every morning, my ears searched for that bark, that smell, and even that fear that he might get loose.

And then Karma got back to us.

The first hit was my health. All my physical activity stopped, and I started to overeat. My weight (well, it wasn't less previously) always hovered around 90. It became 110! My belly was like my wife's when she was in her seventh month of Pregnancy. As I didn't have to take my dog out in the evening and my workload also increased slowly—slowly without noticing—I started coming home late.

My wife's office was nearby, so she could reach home early, but now all the household chores fell on her, and most of the time, when I got home, both of them were asleep. As a result, our relationship took a hit, and there were more disagreements and fighting.

My frustration level began to rise, and then I was introduced to men's best friend "Whiskey." I had it previously, but it was infrequent.

It started with one glass before coming home, and then I didn't know how, but it became a habit. Most of the time, Radhika was asleep. She never caught me, but one day she did.

"Are you drunk?"

"Nooo..."

"Yes ... that smell ....."

"It's a small party, dear... there is nothing to worry about."

And then I fell on the ground, she started sobbing, and my kid was standing. I could see his feet before blacking out.

But the worst was yet to come.

After that incident, our fights increased, my work hours increased further, and my stress and drinking too increased. Our parents got worried. I received angry calls daily from my mother; her father tried to put some sense in me, and her mother just stopped talking to me.

Then, one day, while in the office around 06:00 pm, my head felt dizzy, and I started to sweat; the dizziness became unbearable. My colleagues took notice and took me to the nearest hospital, where my blood pressure was very high. They gave me some medicine, and I left for home.

I returned to the house at 08:30 pm; the whole way, I was feeling worried about my health and what was happening. I hadn't called Radhika because I didn't want her to worry. On reaching my colony, I saw a crowd of around twenty people outside our building, and I saw my wife holding my kid with some policemen around her. Someone tried to break into our house. The lady looking after my son took him and ran outside. She called my wife immediately. Later, we learned that she was the mastermind of this.

My wife was so scared she looked at me and started to cry,

"We have been punished, Rishi, for leaving an innocent kid. Nothing of this sort would have ever happened if he was here."

"Rishi?"

"Yes..."

"You said you would bring stars and moons for me before marriage."

"Yes"

"Please bring him back for me..."

"Hooman left me..."

"Hooman left meeee.."

"Come back..."

"Is this my car... Is this my hooman..."

"Stupid neighbour... always crying..... oooooo I miss u too hooman...."

"Hungry..... food where is it..........."

"Noooo don't hit me... I want food......"

"Water...... some water....."

"PEE, please take me out..... take me out... I don't want to do here...."

"Wait...Where am I going...This aint my Hooman...."

"Hooomannnnnn....."

Twenty-Five

DOING THE RIGHT THING IS HARD.

"Attention all the passengers travelling to Mumbai, please proceed for boarding from Gate no 6."

"Ohh, let them say there is time," Aditya said, looking at Meenakshi.

"Yes, please."

This was all I wanted to hear; still, my rational self tried to reason.

"But Radhika.."

"I don't know anything; all the time, we were scared that anything might happen to our kid. He might get bitten, but there hasn't been one incidence in which he has shown any aggression towards the baby. What did we do? We just left him; it was our fault that we couldn't train him, and he paid the price."

Still, I continued to protest that old dogs and toddlers don't get along, and Kabir has started to walk and is always running around the house.

"We will put baby gates and separate one area for him, and when any house help comes, he will be in his area, and he already has no problem with it. My baby could have been harmed today..." she started crying uncontrollably.

I hugged her and said, "Don't worry; I promise I will bring him back."

As my sister said that day, "It's not whether you have made the right decision. It's about what you make of the decision." So I decided to leave for Silchar, my head was going one way and my heart the other.

I knew getting him back would be hard; I kept on having negative thoughts like he would not be in a good condition. I could bring him back by train or again via flight, but there was no direct train or flight; Jodhpur and Silchar are on opposite sides of the country, with the distance being more than 3000 km, so via road, it will be very hectic. On top of that, how will he react when he reaches our house? How will we segregate the baby and the dog?

But in my heart, I was excited and relieved, I was bringing my hero back.

And you know what? Doing the right thing is hard. The moment I stepped on my flight, all my enthusiasm now has turned into anxiety.

Karma was about to hit me again.

As I landed in Silchar, I realised I hadn't contacted the dog hostel where I had left Chuggi; in all that madness, I had just forgotten about that.

I called him as soon as I sat in my cab.

"Dada, how are you?"

"How's Chuggi?"

"Chuggi? Ohh, that always barking black dog, he is fine."

"I am coming to take him."

"Err what.... Ehh.... Sorry, your voice is breaking." The phone was abruptly disconnected. I tried calling him again but was greeted by the message. The phone number you are calling is currently switched off. Please try calling later.

My heart skipped a beat; maybe his battery died.

I had booked a cab to the 'hostel', where I left him, around 30 km from the airport. I kept on calling him back, but I got the same response.

After one hour, I reached the location; the gate of the premises was locked from the inside. I rang the bell, and all the dogs inside started barking. No one came out, so I strained my ears for Chuggi's shrill bark that he gives whenever I go to pick him up, but it wasn't there. I tried calling him by name, but there was still no response. My heart sank; something didn't feel right.

Then, after 15 minutes of continuous ringing the bell and shouting, a man came out.

"What happened? "

"I want my dog Chuggi, that small black dog that resembles a German Shepherd and Husky."

"That one, I don't know……" he just left.

"Hey, where are you going? Come back... Where the hell is my dog? I pay monthly rent to keep him here; where is my dog?"

All the dogs started barking like anything; they realised something was foul, and then the Dog Hostel owner came.

"Hey, why are you creating trouble here? Who are you?"

"I left my dog Chuggi with you. I paid Rs Ten Thousand upfront and Rs Five Thousand monthly rent. Where is my dog? I want him back."

"You left him here to die, and now you are making all these false claims; I am not responsible for your dog. When you don't know how to keep your dog, why bother me."

"But I am paying money to you, dammit."

"I don't know anything about that. Go away, or these dogs are not held tightly."

"I don't know anything; I want my dog!"

"You accuse me of stealing your money and making foul claims in front of my customers. Wait!"

And then he opened his gate, and one of his German Shepherds came running straight towards me. I quickly turned and ran. The hostel was located on a small but busy street. Amid the chaos of that street, where the blaring horns and shouts of vendors were creating a cacophony, I dashed frantically through the narrow lanes. My breath came in ragged gasps as the snarling German Shepherd lunged closer, its powerful jaws snapping at my heels. I stumbled, and in a flash, the dog's teeth sank into my leg, sending a sharp pain shooting through my body as blood began to seep through my trousers. I cried out in agony, trying to shake the dog off, but the beast held firm. When all seemed lost, my taxi driver, watching in horror, sprang from the vehicle and rushed over, swinging his bag and yelling. The distraction was enough—the dog released its grip, and I was, bloodied but still alive, staggered into the cab, slamming the door behind me.

People gathered around me. The owner of the dog hostel also came and started shouting at me in Bengali.

"I just want my dog back! I shouted... My voice was trembling with anger."

And he just went away muttering something.

I didn't have any proof that I had left Chuggi with him. Typically, these hostels don't give any receipts. He had given me the account number of some random person to whom I was transferring funds, so I had no proof that I left Chuggi with him.

I sat in the car and cried, clueless about where my dog went.

My driver didn't say anything but took pity on me and took me to a hospital. I was injected and bandaged. He said, " Sir, let me take you to a nice tea stall; I haven't seen anyone so desperate for their dog. Please, sir, have some tea with me."

My driver, 'Basanta', took me to a nice tea stall in the Ramnagar area, which made great bread fritters and was famous in that area. It was evening, and the shop was crowded. As I sat in the stall sipping my tea, I couldn't help but wonder what had just happened. I was severely hurt, and I couldn't bring myself to talk about it to my wife or anyone in my family. The experience was overwhelming, especially with everything else going on at home. Did I come all this way just to be bitten by some random dog? It felt like there was no hope, as the owner didn't cooperate, and I had no other leads to find Chuggi.

As I was leaving, a man came and sat near me.

"Sir, I saw you there near Kennel Ashiyana. I worked there until last month but left due to payment issues; the owner is evil, always behind money, and he never used to pay me on time. You know he beat the dogs that came for boarding whenever they barked and sometimes didn't even give them food. People leave them here because you don't have many options in Silchar. I worked in Mumbai and came here to Silchar, my home town, during the COVID times. In Mumbai, the dog hostels were more professional; I worked with one where even celebrity dogs were coming, and he gave facilities like live CCTV. After coming to Silchar, I started working here, but maybe it's time to return to Mumbai; I had a bad experience working with this man who doesn't even fear God. He is evil, sir."

"Wait, you worked there?" I looked at him and thanked the Gods because maybe now I could find Chuggi.

"Oh, yes... and your dog was that black one. He was so dangerous, always ready to bite. But he was very cooperative, too, and never cried, as though he knew you would come back."

"So you know what happened to him? Do you know where he is ?" I took a Rs 500 note from my purse and gave it to him.

"Thank you. All I know is this that he sold him a few days after you went."

"What! But I was even giving him money to keep him."

"Sir, I told you he is a man with no morals."

"So, do you know the person to whom he sold my dog?"

"No, sir, but I know one thing: that person who lives around Sonapur, Meghalaya and has a huge property. He was looking for a guard dog."

That was so vague. Sonapur is 90 km from Silchar, in the Hills of Meghalaya, a small town in the East Jaintia district. The person lived around Sonapur as per him, not even in Sonapur.

In addition, there would be language issues. The population is sparse, and the area is surrounded by dense forest. Finding this person without his name and address would be very difficult. On top of that, I was bitten, so I had to have my anti-rabies vaccination, and right now, I can't even walk properly.

It might be easy in a city, but trying such a thing in a location like this would be foolish. I remembered the movie Finding Nemo, in which a small clownfish father just started a journey to find his son, who he knew was in Sydney.

But it was a movie.

I finished my tea, and a small dog came near me. It looked at me with big eyes, asking for a treat—the same look Chuggi gives when he wants his treats.

I bought him some biscuits, patted him, took my bag, and signalled to Basanta that it was time to leave.

"So, sir, shall we return to the airport?"

Looking at the dog enjoying his biscuits, I realised that love has no limit. I love my dog like my son, and he was missing, movie or no movie; I was ready to search the heavens for him.

"No, Basanta."

Twenty-Six

WHERE ARE YOU?

My first thought was where to start. I needed a plan.

Basanta volunteered to help me and stay with me. We stayed at Silchar the first day, figuring out how to find him in Sonapur. The problem was that language would be an issue, and being a remote place, we didn't know where and how to start. He suggested a nice hotel near Sonapur, on the Guwahati SIilchar Highway, 'Hotel Chilli & Sweet.'

"Mmm, Sahabji, What's your plan? In this big area, it will be impossible to find your Dog," Basanta asked me candidly while chewing tobacco.

"Hmm, that's what I was thinking. Firstly, I will print out his photographs and paste them everywhere. I hope the man who bought him, upon seeing it, will call me and return my dog to me, or someone who might know where the dog is or saw him will call us."

He spit his tobacco and looked at me with disbelief: " Sir, have you seen that place? You have gone mad. I suggest you pack your bag and leave. Bhabhiji is also getting worried. She called me yesterday. You gave her my number. She told me to get you back safely, and you didn't even tell her about getting bitten. She was outraged. Sir, leave this is stupidity and go home." He took out another tobacco pouch and popped it in his mouth.

"Wait, you told her? That's why she called me in the morning, but I couldn't pick it up; I will explain to her on the way. And well, you are right. The plan is too farfetched. I don't know how many posters to print, and I have just seen this place once while going to Guwahati and stopping at the bridge to click photos. There is a jungle out there, and there is also a chance that the person who bought Chuggi might decide not to return him. So I suggest we will start from the local police station."

Basnata spit his tobacco again and smiled, showing all his tobacco-stained teeth or whatever remained of them. "Have you ever gone to any police station? And that's too in Meghalaya. Sir, you have gone crazy. You are not going to find him there. But I like you, so I will take you."

"And also because I am paying you."

Well, he was correct; there was a good chance that this plan might fail. The chances of success were slim, and I will be honest I also had second thoughts.

The next day, we left for Sonapur, Meghalaya, from Silchar. It would be a four-hour drive, but as soon as the hills started, I realised it would be challenging. Few villages were on the route, and Meghalaya is relatively less densely populated. On top of that, the hills were big, and it was raining heavily. To make matters worse, a landslide happened, and we were stuck in traffic for more than six hours.

Just before Sonapur, we found a small temple on the right side of the road. On the left side, there was a massive gorge, a dense forest up the hill behind the Temple, and no one around for miles. I stopped there, prayed, and gave the Priest the photo of my dog and my number just in case he saw him.

He looked at me, shook his head, and gave a small laugh but didn't say anything and stuck the photo outside the temple. As It was already getting dark, we went towards our stay in the Hotel.

The hotel was on the highway near a few cement factories. During the night, it continued raining and was cold, too. The place was very wet and cold. My anxieties regarding Chuggi were preventing me from sleeping, and on top of that, in the middle of the night, I thought I heard some voices; the place seemed spooky.

The following day, the scene from my hotel mesmerised me: lush green hills all around. And then the absurdity of my plan hit me. It would be very difficult to find him here. I don't know the language, culture, or anything else. Sonapur doesn't even seem like a town. Where will I go? And I have come here because a random man said my dog is not even here but around here. This was madness.

As I walked around the area, I came across a beautiful trail going up in the mountains; the mist hung heavy in the hills, shrouding everything in a ghostly haze. After reaching a certain height , I saw the valley below, covered with clouds, and I suddenly felt the urge to shout my dog's name into the open. Emotions overwhelmed me, and tears welled up in my eyes as I called for my dog. 'I'm sorry, please come back, Chuggi! Chuggi, please come back. Do you want your bone? Chuggi, I'm sorry. Look, I have your favourite bone. Please come back.'

My voice echoed off the cliffs, but there was no answering bark, only the soft patter of rain and the rustle of leaves. My heart was pounding with fear and worry. Every crackle of a branch or distant sound filled me with a fleeting hope, only to leave me hollow when I realised there was no sign of him.

My dog was somewhere here, and I had to find him.

Standing there looking at the vast green expanse, I realised crying and doubting myself would not solve my problem, and this was not the way to find him; the world didn't care about what I was feeling or doing. Yes, what I was doing seemed foolish, but it was about my dog. The only way to find him was to look for him, be it in a village or a city.

He is my kid, and I have to find him.

So Basanta and I went straight to the local police station. Firstly, there was no one in that station. It was a small town, and nothing much happened there. After a long time of waiting, someone came. He listened to us but was not sympathetic. He laughed and said, "Who would go look out for a dog? And that's too here." But he suggested we ask the village headman of the neighbouring villages. Disheartened, we left the station. The question was, which village? How would I communicate with the locals when even these guys had difficulty understanding Hindi and English?

We came out and sat in a tea stall. Basanta was eating his tobacco, and I had my tea. I was disappointed; it seemed like I again hit a dead end. My leg was also paining; I didn't know what to do. Suddenly, it became very dark, as though it would rain heavily.

"Basanta, how much I owe you?" I asked, trying to break the silence.

He was looking down at his phone, scrolling through social media. Without lifting his head, he said, "Mmm,"

And then he brought his phone near me and said. " Mmm... ?"

"Basanta , I can't understand this Mmm language."

"MMMMM", and he thrusted his phone in my hand.

Basanta was showing me his Facebook feed. Someone had captured my struggle at the Dog hostel and posted it online.

My silver lining was there; I needed just this. My hopes rose again; maybe this was possible. The power of social media is enormous. I forwarded the same video to my Facebook and Instagram pages with a plea to help me find my dog. Then, it started pouring heavily, and we rushed to our vehicle.

For a few moments, I felt good. Then, looking around at the beautiful mountains and rivers with greenery as far as the eye could see, it hit me that none of my Facebook or Instagram contacts or friends were in Meghalaya. The post was shared locally in Silchar. If my dog had been in Silchar, it could have helped me, but there was no chance here.

"Basanta , but who will see this post here? It's useless."

"Mmm." Spitting his tobacco outside, he said, "Sir, at least it's something. Be happy; you have gone crazy. In the morning, you were so excited and thrilled, like you had seen some beautiful girl, and now again, this ?"

"You have no chance. You are wasting money. I suggest visiting some waterfalls here, and then we will leave." He popped his next pouch in his mouth.

I could hear the heavy raindrops falling on the car. I told Basanta to take me back to the hotel.

A few minutes later, my phone rang.

"Sir, you are here in Silchar and didn't even bother to call me." This was my subordinate Chandra; he was my first subordinate, and I was his first boss. We shared a special bond. When you are a new boss, you play cool, and luckily, you get a very sincere subordinate who does more work than you expect. And where you can share all your experiences. You are also carefree as you are not high in the office hierarchy. On top of that, he was very resourceful, too. He's a charming boy and our small office heartthrob.

"Chandra, I didn't want to bother you because of some personal issues."

"Sir, this is not the way; you have completely alienated me. We have worked together for so long, and you didn't even call me once, I read your post,

You are in so much trouble. Sir, tell me where you are. I am coming right now."

"Thanks, Dude, but there is no need, and right now, I am in Meghalaya. Please don't..."

"Location, sir. "

I couldn't say no to him, so I gave him my location and explained my situation. I felt relieved that he called because I desperately needed help here. But honestly, I had very little hope that he would come. He was coming from Karimganj, which is another 30 kilometres from Silchar.

But the following day, Chandra was there, and he wasn't alone. He also brought his friend, Alex, who was a local of this area. I felt my problems would finally be solved. Sometimes, you need reassurance and a little support to endure difficult situations.

We started our search from Alex's village, Shymplong, near Sonapur, a beautiful village where we even hired some local kids. The locals agreed to help us and even guided us where to go.

We stuck posters of my Dog at all the prominent locations in the villages nearby; in just two days, we posted his posters in more than 100 locations.

My phone rang continuously; most were crank calls, as anyone who saw a black dog would call me. But still, we went to all the caller locations. It was very fun but tiring. Alex did most of the talking; the people of Meghalaya are very warm and fond of talking. Alex would speak for half an hour in the local dialect. To us, it seemed that this person knew exactly where my dog was, but upon asking Alex, he would say that this person also had no idea.

The roads were never good, and hiking was involved in difficult places. My bite wound was troubling me, but I continued. Then, one day, we received a call from the head man of a village named Kuliyang saying that there was one person who had seen your dog; he seemed ferocious, so he initially didn't approach him, but these people live deep in the forest, so a dog was no match for them. They caught him, and now he was in his house.

This description matched my dog. I asked him if he could send his photo on WhatsApp, but he said there is no network at that location, and he is a poor man, and his house is located at a two-hour trek from his village; we would have to go with him there.

The following day, we accompanied the headman to that man's house. We went through lush rice fields with betel nut trees and the rest of the dense jungle. Only a handful of people lived there. We went from one rice field to another and came across a huge mountain. The headman told us that if we went through this mountain, we would reach it in half an hour and take more than two hours to go around it.

I had no option. My leg was paining, and the whole area was damp and cold. No one was around, not even birds. The entire place was so desolate and empty.

The headman's half-hour was, as per his stamina, but for us, it would be more than Two hours; the Mountain was steep, with huge rocks and boulders and dense undergrowth. As we started our trek, I felt a tingle in my legs, and overlooking it, I continued, holding one tree or rock. I lost my footing sometimes, climbing on rocks somehow with the help. I managed to go about fifty meters, and then checked my feet. The sight was not good, there were leeches on it sucking my blood; I looked at it and then at the climb ahead, where have I come?

The headman smiled at me, saying it was not far; hold on. I did my best to remove the leeches and continued, and then, finally, somehow, we reached the top of the mountain. Now, I don't remember how we came down; I only remember more pain and a lot of slipping. The angle on this side of the mountain was steeper than we climbed. We crossed one small stream and continued. Finally, after two hours of this ordeal, we reached that place.

As I saw the villager, he smiled at mc, and I fainted.

Next, I found myself on a small cot, given herbs by the villager and headman. My phone was out of network, so I realised my family would be very worried.

And then I heard a bark.

My heart skipped a beat. There was another bark, and the barking increased. It was an excited bark.

My boy was here; he was here.

I got up with some help and went straight to the voice with tears in my eyes.

"So you finally found him?" Meenakshi asked.

"Hooman??"

"Hooman.. Hooman??"

"My Hooooomannn............"

Twenty-Seven

AT LAST...

"No..."

"All passengers from rows 21 to 40, please proceed for boarding."

There was silence. I shifted in my seat, took my bag, and said, "I think it's time for goodbye."

"You are a good man, Rishi. I don't know what to say; I believe Chuggi is happy wherever he is." Shivani said. "He is happy."

"What does this mean you found him?"

I looked at the line and said, "This is not the end of the story."

Shivani stood from her seat and said, "You stop right here. I am not allowing you to leave before completing the story. If possible, I will give you a discount on our airline if this leaves."

Meenakshi looked at the line and said, "There is still some time ..."

Aditya held his head and said, " Bro, where is your dog now? Just complete this story. This plane will leave." He stood up and picked up his bag.

Meenakshi gave him a look, and he looked again at the boarding gate and sat back.

"Hurry, man. We have a plane to board."

It was another dog who was barking; he was black and looked a bit like him; the experience was too much for me; I was hurt and broken. My leg's condition was deplorable. So Basanta took me straight to a hospital in the nearest town, Khileriat, to get it checked.

I had tried everything, but there was still no news of Chuggi's whereabouts. I searched every corner of the area. I attempted to call the pet boarding place again to ask him to share the address with me. However, he was upset with me due to the negative media attention and refused to provide the details. Chandra said he couldn't afford any more leaves, so he and Alex decided to leave in a day.

I didn't share anything about this incident with my wife. But my family was also getting impatient and nervous. I had my job, and my kid was missing his father, and here I was out there looking for an old dog in the middle of nowhere.

I knew now that nothing could be done; it was time I accepted reality. Anyhow, the fundamental problem would still remain even if I found him. My kid is still very small, the Dog is ferocious, and the house is also small, and after this experience, I was unsure how Chuggi would behave.

And in the end, life is not a movie.

Feeling disheartened, I decided to leave with Chandra and Alex.

At around 01:00 pm, my phone rang.

"Is this Mr Rishi?"

"Yes," I replied

"I saw a poster for a lost dog named Chuggi. Are you his original owner?"

This statement made my heart skip a beat. He knew where my Dog was!

"Yes, I am his original owner."

"Mr Rishi, you left your dog at Kennel Ashiyana at Tarapur in Silchar, right."

"Yes, Yes, that's right," I replied enthusiastically.

"My name is Phawa. I live in Shillong and have one house at Lumshnong village near Sonapur. I already have two dogs, but theft has still occurred at my premises, so I was looking for another dog, preferably a guard dog. My friend at Silchar owns Kennel Ashiyana, and I learned about your dog through him. He said his owner left him.

He is a good guard dog and is up for adoption. I liked him immediately and bought him here."

"You should have never left him there, such a beautiful young dog; his eyes were so sad. If you can't take care of a dog, why leave him? So many dogs are left daily. He had no one other than you. The poor boy always missed you."

"Yes, you are right. But now I want him back; he is family. I will pay you all the expenses, but please give me back my Dog."

"You got a bit late, Mr Rishi. Even at this age, your dog was very active, confident, and always on alert. We liked him from day one, but even with all the love, he never really became part of our family; he was always waiting at the door. He won't go out even if the door was left ajar by mistake, waiting for you to come and take him."

"So what happened to him? Is he alright?"

"A white Swift Dezire car pulled up near our house a few days ago. He started barking loudly. We tried to calm him down, but he still kept barking. As the car drove away, your dog, who was at the gate, ran after it. This was unusual because, as I said, he never went out, even if the door was open. Unfortunately, the gate was also not bolted properly that day. We tried to catch up with him but lost sight of him around a turn. Then yesterday, I saw a poster of him in front of the temple near the Sonapur Tunnel and called you."

Wait. I was travelling in a white Swift Dezire. I didn't know what to say to him, which meant my Dog ran after me. I thanked him, asked for his address, and left for that place.

My Dog was out there searching for me.

The question was, where would he go? If he was after me, he would follow the scent of the vehicle, and with mountains and the highway traffic, he might get badly hurt or worse. But still, the dog's sense of smell is very keen he might find me, and I had come this far; there was no going back now. I decided I would try my best to find him. The most logical thing is that if he was following the scent of my vehicle, he should come to Chilli & Sweet. I informed the guard to keep notice, and if any dog with Chuggi's description went near the car, he would call me. Meanwhile, Basanta arranged another vehicle, and we left for Lumshnong.

We arrived at Lumshnong, but he wasn't there. After searching the entire village, we retraced our steps back to Chilli & Sweet, asking people and small shop owners if they had seen him, but with no luck. The Guwahati-Silchar Highway was bustling with activity, and my heart sank at the thought of my poor pup possibly running after my vehicle on that mountainous highway. I couldn't shake the feeling that something might have happened to him because of my carelessness, and I felt an overwhelming sense of guilt. As a God-fearing man and a firm believer in Karma, I asked for forgiveness. We reached Chilli & Sweet, but he was still nowhere to be found, so we decided to continue. Eventually, we came across a small road leading up to a hill from the highway, where BSF guards were stationed. We stopped and showed them a photo of my dog.

One enthusiastically said he saw this dog going up this hill. We asked him if we could go there. He said the mountain forms a boundary between India and Bangladesh and is a sensitive area. He only allowed us to go to a small forest check post one kilometre from that location.

After some formalities, we took the road through the mountains. Lush green forests were on one side, and a steep gorge was on the other side of the road. A beautiful River was flowing deep down the valley, going all the way to the plains of Bangladesh.

Our car could not go up to the forest check post; the road was deplorable, and again, it started raining. We trekked for some time, and then I left Chandra, Basnata and Alex and went up further by myself. The forest was on both sides of the road, and no one was around for miles. I was getting nervous. One, it was a border area; two, a national forest filled with animals and snakes; three, my leg was paining again; and finally, the heavy rains and, this time, a strong wind was also accompanying it.

A small trail was going through the dense forest that went straight to the forest checkpoint, about 100 meters uphill. I decided to go up there and see if the person at that post had seen Chuggi. The rain poured down heavily as I walked through the dark forest. Each step was a struggle, with the mud pulling at my boots. Lightning flashed, casting eerie shadows that danced among the twisted trees. The wind howled, and its mournful cries echoed through the desolation. I felt like unseen creatures were lurking in the underbrush, and my heart pounded as the cold seeped into my bones. Suddenly, a branch snapped behind me. I spun around, breathless, but saw nothing. Drenched and shivering, I pressed on, with every rustle and crack sending chills down my spine, praying to escape this. Somehow, I reached the checkpoint, but there was no one there.

I was disappointed and angry with myself; why was this ordeal not ending?

Then, on my way back, I stumbled down the slippery hill; the ground gave way beneath me. I lost my footing and tumbled in a blur of wet leaves and sharp rocks. Pain exploded in my leg as I crashed to the bottom, a jagged rock tearing into my flesh, and that's too in the same leg that was paining. Gasping, I clutched my leg, feeling the warm blood mix with the cold rain. The pain was excruciating, radiating up my body. I tried to stand, but my leg buckled, sending me back into the mud. Panic set in as I realised I was trapped, injured and alone in this relentless storm, far from help.

I picked myself up and continued. As I limped and bled while coming down and somehow reached the main road, lush green forests extended as far as my eye could see; on any other given day, I would have loved to be there, but at that moment, I felt lonely and broken both physically and mentally.

And I just wanted my dog.

Just as I was about to give up again, on the road below from where I was standing, I saw a dog with a tail like Chuggi.

My heart skipped a beat. Is this Chuggi? Or is fate playing with me again? It was too far to tell. It could well be any animal, probably a monkey, but... No, it was him. Without thinking, I again rushed down that hill, in the same condition, toward that dog like a mad person, shouting Chuggi! Chuggi. The angle was too steep; I slipped and rolled downwards, and my head hit a tree. And then everything became black.

I don't remember when it happened, but only that I had pain in my head, blood in my mouth, and some voices of people shouting.

Luckily, a few locals saw me there and called Basanta and Chandra. Basanta took me straight to Silchar; he took that risk because there was no good hospital nearby, and more importantly, he felt I was going mad.

I woke up in a hospital after four days; my wife was standing next to me. She was very scared and upset.

"I saw him. He was there on the road."

"Rishi, what is this? Your leg could have been amputated; this madness ends here. This is not some fantasy; it's real life. You have a son. Before doing all this, you didn't even think of him about me once? We are going home. You tried everything. Please, let's go home." she started crying. "I don't want to see you like this; it's all my fault. I should have never asked you to come here."

"But...." I realised I was so close to finding him, seeing tears in my wife's eyes, I finally gave up, and we decided to leave as soon as I got discharged.

I got discharged in a few days. Our flight was scheduled to leave at 03:00 pm that evening; before leaving Silchar, we thought we should visit the Shiv temple near our house to pray for forgiveness and good health for our Dog.

My heart was filled with so many emotions; my mind was playing a flashback movie of my dog, like when I saw him playing with those colony kids for the first time, and as I walked by, he saw me and started to follow me, that frail small Dog. He used to sit in front of the room heater on those cold nights, those nights when he used to cry and disturb our sleep, those eyes that lit up whenever he got a treat.

Just like that, we reached our last house location.

We gave a quick look at the house and proceeded to the temple.

It was busy as usual; it was 01:30 in the afternoon.

As we came out of the temple. I took one last view of the location: those old street dogs who used to run away at just one slight growl of Chuggi.

"Sir, you will miss your flight if we don't leave now." The taxi driver shouted.

My heart was saying dude, wait; your Dog would be somewhere near. Don't go.

But, It was over. My dog wasn't coming back, I had already tried everything.

And then a thought stroked me: if Chuggi was there at that mountain and if he followed the scent of my car, he could come to Silchar, and here he might find his way to his old house; if he did that, he would surely visit one person.

Munni.......

I left Radhika and Kabir in the car and ran towards the Chicken shop. I knew I had to find Munni; she was our last hope.

I started searching for her frantically.

And then, on that busy street, I heard a faint bark, like a dog asking for something, and then one more, a bark of a dog missing something or someone; in between all the car horns and traffic, I recognised that bark, the bark that I wanted to hear, the bark of my Dog.

My Dog was here. He stood thirty feet away with cars and people whooshing away, his head tilted and his body shaking rapidly. He barked loudly again and ran towards me like a bullet. I had found my pup. Chuggi was here.

Epilogue

We said goodbye to Shivani and rushed to our plane; Meenakshi was sitting at 15 a, and believe it or not, Aditya had seat 15 b.

As for me, I was sitting in the back. At 27 f. After take-off, both of them came to my seat.

"I was wondering, how was your dog when you met him near the chicken shop ?" said Meenakshi

"Even after running after my car and travelling for more than a Hundred kilometres, he was fit and fine; only his legs hurt a bit from all that running. He was there for the last four days. Initially, he sat outside my old building and then shifted to the Chicken Shop. As per the chicken shop owner, all the dogs had been side-lined, and he was the undisputed king of the area. Was he happy there or